TALES OF LONG AGO

TALES OF
LONG AGO

Retold by

Enid Blyton

Illustrated by
ANNE and JANET JOHNSTONE

DEAN & SON Ltd.
PRINTED IN   GREAT BRITAIN
41/43 Ludgate Hill   LONDON EC4

Made and Printed in Great Britain by Purnell & Sons, Ltd.
Paulton (Somerset) and London

603 03261 3

Contents

TALES OF ANCIENT GREECE

TALES FROM THE ARABIAN NIGHTS

CONTENTS

TALES OF ANCIENT GREECE

Pandora and the Whispering Box

LONG, LONG ago, when the world was new, and no pain or sorrow was known, Epimetheus lived with his beautiful young wife Pandora. They dwelt in a house made of branches and leaves, for the sun shone always, and the wind was never cold.

Every one was happy. Merry voices came on the breeze, and laughter was heard everywhere. Epimetheus and Pandora were happiest of all, for they loved one another very dearly, and were never apart.

One day, as they were dancing beneath the trees, they saw the god Mercury coming towards them. He carried a wooden box on his shoulder, and looked tired and hot.

"Ask him what he has in that box," said Pandora to Epimetheus. But Mercury would not tell them.

"That is not for you to know," he answered. "Will you permit me to put my box in your dwelling and leave it there for a while? I have far to go, and the weight of it makes my steps slow. I will call for it on my way back."

"We will take care of it for you," said Epimetheus. "Put it in a corner of our house. It will be safe there."

"Do not open it," said Mercury warningly. "You will never cease to regret it, if you do."

"We shall not even look at it," said Epimetheus. "You need not fear, Mercury."

So the god placed his box on the ground in a corner of Pandora's dwelling. Then, bidding the two farewell, he set off again through the forest.

Pandora was filled with curiosity to know what was in the box. She left Epimetheus to dance with his companions, and stole into the house alone. She looked at the box for a long time, and then her eyes opened wide in astonishment.

The box was whispering! Little sighs and tiny sounds came from it. Pandora felt more curious than ever. There must be something alive inside to make that whispering noise.

She ran to the box and knelt down by it. It was very beautiful, made of finely-wrought dark wood, and on the top was a prettily carved head that seemed to smile at Pandora. Round the box was a strong golden cord, tied in a tight knot.

The whispering went on and on. Pandora listened, but she could not hear what was said. Her fingers trembled to undo the cord—but just then Epimetheus came in to beg her to come and play with him.

"Oh, Epimetheus, I wish I knew what was in this box," said Pandora longingly. "Do you think I might just peep?"

Epimetheus was shocked.

"Mercury said that we were not to know," he said. "Come away, Pandora. Come and play with me in the sunshine, where every one is happy."

But Pandora would not go. Epimetheus looked at her in surprise, and then, thinking that she would surely come if he left her alone, he ran out to his comrades.

Pandora heard the laughter and shouts of her friends, but she thought of nothing but the whispering box. Would it matter if she just undid the golden cord? Surely she could do that without harm.

She looked round to see if Epimetheus was really gone, then she turned eagerly to the box. Her clever fingers worked at the golden cord, but it was so tight that she could not loosen it for a long time.

"Pandora, Pandora, come and dance!" cried her com-

Epimetheus danced with his companions

panions outside. But the maiden would not answer. She must undo the cord; she could not be happy until she had.

She pulled it and shook it. The knot was tight and difficult to untie. Pandora almost gave it up. Then suddenly it loosened, and swiftly she undid it. The golden cord slid on to the floor—and there lay the box, ready to open at a touch.

"Now that I have undone the cord, it is stupid not to open the box," thought the maiden. "Shall I just lift up the lid, peep inside, and then let it drop? What harm could that do to any one? I really must find out what makes the whispering noise."

She put her ear to the lid, and listened. Then, quite clearly, she heard tiny voices.

"Pandora, sweet Pandora!" they said. "Let us out, we pray you! Our prison is so dark and gloomy, will you not free us?"

The maiden was astonished. Should she free whatever was inside? As she was trying to make up her mind, she heard Epimetheus coming again. She knew he would not let her peep, but would tie up the box, so she hurriedly lifted up the lid to look inside before he came.

Alas! Within the box were crammed all the sorrows, pains, and evils of the world! As soon as Pandora lifted the lid, out they all flew, tiny brown-winged creatures like moths. They flew to Pandora and the surprised Epimetheus, and stung them. At once the two felt pain and anger for the first time. Then the brown-winged creatures flew out into the forest, and fastening themselves on to the merry-makers there, changed their cries of happiness to pain and dismay.

Epimetheus and Pandora began to quarrel. Pandora wept bitterly, and Epimetheus scolded her angrily for opening the box. In the midst of their quarrel, they suddenly heard a sweet voice calling to them. They stopped their angry words to listen.

The voice came from the box, which Pandora had hurriedly shut as soon as the brown-winged creatures had flown out. It was a high voice, sweet and loving.

"Let me out, let me out!" it cried. "I will heal your sorrows, and bring you peace! Only let me out!"

"Shall I open the box again?" said Pandora.

"Since you cannot do much worse mischief than you have done already, you may as well see what is left," said Epimetheus gloomily.

So for the second time Pandora opened the box, and this time out flew, not a brown-winged creature, but a little snowy-winged spirit. She was called Hope, and had been crammed in at the bottom of all the evil creatures. It was her duty to heal the wounds made by them, and to cheer those whom they had visited.

She flew at once to Pandora and Epimetheus, and brushing the wounds on their skin with her snowy wings, she healed them. Then off she flew to do the same for their unhappy companions outside.

And thus, because of Pandora's foolish curiosity, sorrow, pain, and evil entered the world, and have been with us ever since. But Hope stayed too, and whilst we have her, we are content.

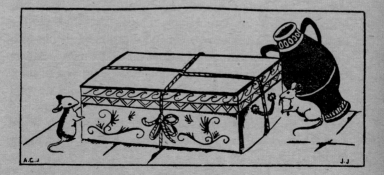

Phaeton and the Sun-Horses

IN A SUNNY corner of Greece there once dwelt a lovely nymph called Clymene. She had a golden-haired son, Phaeton, and when the yellow sunshine played on his hair, she would laugh and say:

"See how your father caresses you, Phaeton!"

"Is my father then the great sun-god?" asked the little boy. "Is it he who drives the golden sun-chariot across the sky each day?"

"It is indeed he," answered Clymene. "You may well be proud of such a father, Phaeton."

The boy was pleased to think that his father was a god. He ran out to tell his playmates. At first they believed him, and listened in wonder. But as the days went by and Phaeton boasted more and more of his wonderful father, his friends became tired.

"Show us some proof that he is indeed your father!" they cried. "We do not believe you, Phaeton. You are a boaster!"

White with anger, the boy ran to his mother.

"They say that the great Apollo is not my father!" he said. "Mother, let me go to him, and ask him to show these unbelievers that I am indeed his son."

"You shall go," said Clymene fondly. "I will tell you the way, and you shall set forth to-morrow."

The next day the boy set out on his long journey. Eagerly he set his face to the east, where the great sun-chariot appeared each morning. Day after day he walked steadily towards Apollo's palace, eager to meet his father and embrace him.

At last he arrived, and stood marvelling at the wonderful palace, whose pillars glittered with gold and precious stones,

Phaeton's Sun-horse

whose ceilings were of ivory, and whose doors were of gleaming silver.

The boy climbed the golden steps to the throne-room, and stopped on the threshold, dazzled by the brightness within. Apollo sat on his glittering throne, with his crown of gleaming sun-rays on his bright head.

Seeing the boy, he took off his crown, and laid it aside, bidding the youth come near him.

"I am your son," said Phaeton proudly. "I come to greet you, oh my father. My playmates scoff at me, and say that I am not your son. I would have you prove it to them, so that I may not feel shame before them."

"You are indeed my son," said Apollo, holding out his arms to the boy, who gladly went to them. "I am your father and all the world shall know, for I will prove it to every one. Ask me any boon you wish, and I will grant it."

"Father, grant that I may drive your sun-chariot to-morrow!" cried Phaeton, delighted to hear what his father said. "Then when my friends on the earth below see me holding the reins, they will look up in wonder and say:

Phaeton asks a boon from Apollo

'See! There is Phaeton in his father's chariot! Now we know that he spoke the truth.' "

A frown darkened the god's forehead, and he shook his head.

"Ask me anything but that, Phaeton, my son," he said. "The horses cannot be guided by any hand but mine. Even stern Jupiter, chief of all the gods, dares not drive my chariot. You do not know what you ask. Choose another boon, and I will grant it."

"I will have nothing else," said the wilful boy, beginning to pout and frown. "A god cannot break his word, my father, and I hold you to yours. Let me drive the sun-horses."

Nothing that Apollo could say would make the boy change his mind, and at last the sun-god gave his consent.

"You will kill yourself," he said. "You are foolish to pay no heed to my warning, but since you will not choose any other boon, I cannot help but grant your wish. See, dawn is near at hand, and the gates of heaven are opening. It is time to mount the sun-chariot, and set forth on the journey through the heavens."

Apollo led his son to the gleaming chariot. The four horses were harnessed to the chariot-pole, and eagerly they pawed the ground, and champed their bits, anxious to be off.

Phaeton leapt into the car and took the reins, whilst Apollo gave him solemn warning.

"Drive along the middle way of the sky," he said, "for the middle course is the safest. If you go too low, you will set the mountain-tops on fire, and if you go too high you will lose your way among the stars. Do not use the whip, for the horses need holding in rather than urging on. Even my strong hand is hardly powerful enough to grasp the reins firmly. As for yours, my son, I fear that it will never hold in such fiery horses—leap down now, I pray you, and let me take your place. It is not too late to change your mind."

But the proud boy would not heed his father's warning. He shook the reins impatiently, and the horses leapt forward. In a moment they were gone.

At first Phaeton remembered all his father had told him. He held the reins tightly, and called the horses by name. But soon the fiery animals felt that the hand holding them was not the strong one to which they were accustomed. They pulled at the reins, and Phaeton could not hold the horses back.

Then they ran wild among the stars, leaving the road they knew, and plunged madly here and there. Phaeton was terrified, and the people on the earth below gazed upwards in horror, frightened to see the sun travelling out of his usual course.

The boy pulled at the reins with all his might. He tried to call the horses, but so great was his fear that he could not remember their names. He dropped the reins, and sank to his knees, holding fearfully to the chariot, which was rocking from side to side.

Then the sun-horses left the stars, and plunged downwards towards the earth. The chariot grazed the mountain-tops and set them on fire. So great was the heat that rivers were dried up, seas grew less, and trees withered and died. Nearer and nearer to the earth went the chariot, and all the people cried out in fear.

The fruitful ground was scorched and withered in great stretches, which became deserts that remain to this day. The people of Africa were burnt black with the awful heat, and never did their skin return to its rightful colour. They have remained black for all time.

The terrified people fell upon their knees and prayed to Jupiter to save them. All their crops were destroyed, and every blade of grass was withered. The very lakes boiled and seethed with the heat, and here and there the earth itself cracked and groaned.

Jupiter heard the cries from the frightened people. Rising from his couch, he looked out through the heavens to see what the tumult was about. When he saw the smoking earth, and caught sight of the sun-chariot plunging downwards, he knew that only he could save the world.

He took a thunderbolt, and hurled it fiercely at the chariot. It struck Phaeton on the shoulder, and he fell to earth, his hair ablaze.

Cygnus was turned into a swan

Then the sun-horses shook off their yokes, and broke loose. They galloped off to find their stalls in the sky, and that day night came early, for the sun shone no more after noonday.

In vain Clymene and Apollo grieved for their foolish little son. He was slain by the thunderbolt, and fell into the river Eridanus. His friend Cygnus dived in to find him, and at last pined away in sorrow. He was turned into a swan, and for many a year swam up and down the waters mourning for the golden-haired Phaeton.

Proserpina and the King of the Underworld

THERE was once a beautiful maiden called Proserpina, who loved to play with the nymphs among the flowers. Her mother, Ceres, was the goddess of agriculture, and worked hard to make the farmers' corn grow well. Often she left her little daughter in the care of the nymphs all day long, but at night, when she returned from her labours, she took Proserpina lovingly in her arms and kissed her, for she loved her daughter better than anything else in the world.

One day Proserpina went to gather flowers with her playmates, the nymphs. She sat on a bank making bright garlands, laughing her silvery laugh, and singing merry songs. The nymphs sat around her, filling her lap with fresh violets.

Suddenly there came the sound of galloping hoofs in the distance, and the nymphs looked to see who drove the horses—but they saw nothing, for trees and bushes hid the nearby carriage.

The dark driver of the galloping horses heard the songs and laughter of the maiden Proserpina. He longed to see who the singer was, so he pulled in his four coal-black horses, leapt down from his carriage, and went to peep through the bushes.

He was Pluto, King of the Underworld, a dark and gloomy monarch, feared by every one. No flowers blossomed in his horrid kingdom, no birds sang, and the sun never shone. His face was stern, and his lips set tightly

Pluto watched the maiden Proserpina

together, for he never smiled. On his dark head he wore a crown, and in his hand he carried a sceptre and a key, to show how carefully he guarded those he took with him to his underground kingdom.

As soon as he saw the beautiful maiden Proserpina sitting happily among the flowers, he fell in love with her, and longed to take her down to his dark kingdom to brighten it. He knew that her mother, Ceres, would never let her marry him, so he made up his mind to capture her straightaway, and carry her off.

He strode through the bushes, and made his way to the surprised maiden. The nymphs leapt up in terror, for they knew Pluto. He caught hold of Proserpina, and picked her up. She screamed and dropped all her flowers in panic, calling for her mother to come and help her.

Pluto knew that if Ceres came he would certainly be forced to let the maiden go, so he ran swiftly to his waiting carriage, leapt into it with Proserpina, shook the reins, and galloped off with her. The black horses rushed away, and soon the frightened maiden could no longer hear the cries and wails of her friends the nymphs.

"Set me free!" she begged. "Let me go back to my mother, who will mourn for me bitterly, for she loves me with all her heart."

"And so do I love you with all my heart," said the dark King tenderly. "I want you to be my Queen, fair Proserpina. You shall sit by my side in my dismal kingdom, and brighten the darkness with your youth and beauty."

But Proserpina was frightened and unhappy. She struggled to get free, and cried aloud for help. Pluto held her tightly, and urged his horses on ever more swiftly. At last they came to the river Cyane, which, hearing the maiden's

Proserpina struggled to get free

cries, reared up its waters angrily, as if it would engulf Pluto
and his horses.

The King saw that it would be folly to enter the raging
waters, and he struck the earth fiercely with his two-pronged
spear. At once a yawning cavern appeared, down which
the horses plunged. Proserpina cried out with fear, and
then, thinking to leave something to show her mother the
way she had gone, she quickly tore off her shining girdle
and flung it to the water-nymph in the river, bidding her
take it to Ceres.

Then the earth closed up, and nothing more was seen of Pluto and his black horses. Only the sound of their galloping feet could be heard echoing far beneath the ground. Not for a moment did the fiery animals pause until they reached the foot of Pluto's throne.

That night Ceres came home from her labours to seek her little daughter. She searched everywhere, and began to weep in fear, when she found the spilt flowers that Proserpina had dropped. She called her by name, but no one answered. All night long the poor mother sought for her daughter, and when day dawned she still wandered on, calling aloud for her.

Day after day Ceres journeyed to find Proserpina. She forgot her duties, and neglected to help the farmers. Grass and corn drooped, and fruit would not ripen. All over the world went the unhappy mother, asking for news of her child, but hearing none.

At last in despair she came back to the land from which she had first set out. She wandered by the banks of the river Cyane, and suddenly the waters cast a shining girdle at her feet. She picked it up with joy—for it was Proserpina's!

"Now I know that my child has been here!" she cried. "I shall find her if I seek long enough."

She hastened on, and soon came to a clear fountain, whose crystal waters gushed up into the air. Ceres sat down by them, weary with her search, and closing her eyes, she listened to the murmuring of the waters.

But suddenly she heard words in the murmuring. The fountain was speaking to her.

"Oh, Ceres, listen to me!" said the nymph of the fountain. "I grieve for you, for I have seen you weep for your lovely daughter. I can tell you where she is."

"Tell me, tell me," begged Ceres.

Ceres picked up Proserpina's girdle

"I draw my waters from dark caverns underground," mumured the nymph. "One day as I rushed along below the earth, I passed near the throne of gloomy Pluto, King of the Underworld. By his side I saw your fair daughter, Proserpina. She is his Queen, O Ceres, but she is not happy, for she longs for sunshine and flowers, the song of birds and the laughter of friends."

Ceres listened is dismay. She was glad to know at last where her child was, but she knew that Pluto would never give her up. Mourning deeply, she went to a cave, and there she wept and sorrowed unseen, forgetting all her duties to men and women.

"Nothing shall grow on the earth whilst my daughter is with Pluto," she vowed. "The world shall mourn with me!"

Then trees and grass died, corn rotted, fruit perished. Hunger came amongst the people, and at last, almost starving, they prayed to Jupiter, King of Heaven, to bring back Proserpina, so that Ceres might once more be happy, and look after their crops for them.

When Ceres heard the prayers of the people she arose and left her cave. She too prayed to Jupiter to allow her daughter to return once more.

Then Jupiter, moved by so many prayers, granted Ceres' wish.

"Proserpina shall come back to earth—but only if she has eaten nothing during her stay in the Underworld," he said.

Joyfully Ceres sent the god Mercury to fetch her daughter. He descended to the dark kingdom, and made his way to Pluto.

"Jupiter bids you send Proserpina back to the sunshine," he said.

"And what more did he say?" asked Pluto, with a grim look.

"Only that if she had eaten anything she could not come," answered Mercury. "But it is well known that Proserpina has refused all food since she has been with you."

Then the bright-haired Queen began to weep and wail bitterly. She held out a pomegranate to Mercury, and showed him where she had sucked some seeds from it.

"Alas! Alas!" she cried. "Only to-day have I accepted from Pluto this pomegranate, O Mercury. Six seeds have I eaten. Must I therefore stay here for ever?"

Mercury sadly made his way back to Jupiter, who sat frowning deeply.

"Return to the Underworld," he commanded Mercury. "Tell Pluto that for every seed Proserpina has eaten, she must stay for a month with him—the rest of the year she may spend with her mother on earth."

Swiftly Mercury returned to Pluto, and gave him Jupiter's message.

"She has eaten six seeds, therefore she must spend six months of each year with me," said the dark King. "I have been kind to her, so she should return willingly to me when the time comes."

Gladly Proserpina arose from her throne, and went to Mercury's side. He carried her up the long, dark way to the sunshine, and there, eager and loving, stood Ceres, her mother, her arms outstretched in welcome.

Proserpina ran to her, and embraced her, overjoyed to see her again. Then the whole world rejoiced with Ceres. The sun shone warmly down, and the clouds fled away. The grass sprang up bright and fresh, new wheat made the fields green, flowers bloomed, and birds sang.

For six months Proserpina lived with her mother, happy and free from care, playing every day in the bright sunshine. Men and women rejoiced, for the world was fruitful,

Pluto and Proserpina

and when harvest-time came, the granaries were full to over-flowing.

But as the half-year drew to an end, the thoughts of Proserpina turned to gloomy Pluto, all alone in his dark kingdom. She knew that he missed her, and longed for her return, for in his own stern and frowning way he loved her dearly.

"I go now to Pluto," she told her mother, when the six

months ended. "Do not grieve, for the King of the Underworld is not unkind to me. I will return again to you at the
end of another half-year."

She went back to Pluto—but Ceres again withdrew to her
cave, and wept and sorrowed for all the months that
Proserpina was away. And once again the world sorrowed

The world mourns each year, when Proserpina has gone

with her, the flowers died, the birds ceased their singing,
and clouds shut out the golden sun.

Year after year the same thing happened. All was sunshine and brightness when Proserpina appeared, and sorrow
and darkness when she went. So we have the beauty and
warmth of summer, when the daughter of Ceres is with us,
and the cold and bitterness of winter when she has departed.
The world rejoices at her return, and mourns when she is
gone.

The Maiden of the Laurel Tree

ONE DAY, as Apollo walked through the forest, he saw Cupid, the little God of Love, playing with his bow and arrows. He stopped by him, and laughed.

"Why do you play with such warlike weapons?" he asked. "Leave such things to me, little god. What harm can you do with those?"

"You cannot harm me with *your* weapons, but I can harm you with mine," answered Cupid. He chose a sharp-pointed, golden arrow, and fitting it to his bow, shot it at Apollo. Then he chose a second arrow, blunt and tipped with lead. This he shot at a lovely maiden, Daphne, the daughter of the river-god.

As soon as the golden arrow struck Apollo he became full of love for Daphne, but she, struck by the leaden arrow, would have none of his wooing. In vain he pleaded with her to marry him; she would not let him come near her.

She was a strong maiden, fair of face, and fond of running and hunting. She wished to marry no one, least of all Apollo. When he fell upon his knees, and begged her to show him mercy, she ran away.

Then Apollo, fierce and full of love, pursued her. She did not fear him at first, for she thought that she could easily outrun him—but soon she saw that he would over-take her, for he was very strong and tireless.

"Do not fly from me!" begged Apollo. "I am no peasant fellow, lovely Daphne. I am Apollo, god of the sun, strong and powerful. Marry me, and we will be happy together."

But Daphne was deaf to his cries. On she went, and on

Cupid was playing with his bow and arrows

and on, panting and fearful. Then, glancing round, she saw that the god had almost caught her up.

Poor Daphne could not run much longer. Swiftly she turned and fled down to the river, calling upon her father to help her.

"Oh, my father!" she cried. "Save me, save me! Change my form, so that Apollo will not know me! I can run no farther!"

The river-god heard her call. Quickly he rose from the waters, and muttered the words that would save his daughter from Apollo.

Then a strange thing happened. The maiden felt her feet rooted to the ground so that she could no longer move them. Her outstretched arms became branches, and round her soft body grew the bark of a tree. Her hair and fingers became leaves waving in the wind—she was changed to a laurel tree!

B

Apollo came rushing up, and flung his arms around her—then he drew back in surprise. It was no maiden he was embracing, but a tree. Soon he saw what had happened, and in grief he kissed the tree, and called it by loving names.

"Sweet Daphne!" he said. "You should not have been so fearful of me. I would not have harmed you. But since you are now lost to me for ever, and cannot be my bride, you shall be my tree. I will wear a crown of your leaves, and when men are crowned conquerors they too shall choose your leaves for wreaths. Both men and gods shall pay you homage. Your leaves shall always be green, and shall never decay!"

So to this day the laurel is evergreen, and, as Apollo promised, its leaves are always chosen for the crowns of conquerors.

Daphne was transformed into a laurel tree

The Watchman with a Hundred Eyes

ONCE Jupiter, King of Heaven, saw a lovely maiden called Io, daughter of the river-god. He admired her very much and came down to earth to visit her. He was afraid that Juno, his wife, would be jealous, and so that she might not see him talking to Io, he caused a thick cloud to hide them from sight.

But one afternoon, Juno, awaking from sleep, looked out from her high window in heaven. She had that day commanded all the clouds to leave the earth, and when she saw one by the river, thick and unmoving, she was filled with wonder.

She descended to earth to find out what made it. Jupiter heard her coming and, swift as thought, changed the river-nymph into a lovely heifer. When Juno swept away the cloud, all she saw was Jupiter by the side of a beautiful cow.

"Why do you need this cloud?" she asked.

"See, I have been creating a lovely heifer," said Jupiter. "Is she not pretty?"

Juno wondered if the heifer had been a nymph. "I will ask Jupiter to give her to me; then if he refuses I shall know that it is no heifer, but a nymph," she thought.

Jupiter did not want to give Juno the heifer, but he could think of no reason to refuse his wife's request. So he handed the heifer over to her, and Juno took her.

She called her watchman, Argus, and when he came she bade him watch over the heifer carefully, and guard her

Io wrote her name with her hoof

so well that Jupiter could not take her away again. Argus promised to obey, and at once sat down by the heifer to watch.

There was no better watchman in the world than Argus, for he had a hundred eyes, and these were never all closed at once. Only one pair was shut at a time, leaving ninety-eight on guard.

Poor Io, amazed at being turned into a heifer, tried to call her father and sisters to her. But her voice had changed to a loud bellow, and terrified her. Her father missed her, and went to seek her, calling her fondly, but getting no reply.

At last he came to the field where the heifer stood, and exclaiming in wonder at such a pretty animal, he went to stroke her. Poor Io! She could not tell him who she was, but she thrust her soft muzzle into his hand, and tried to speak to him with her great eyes.

Then suddenly she thought that she would write her name in the earth with her hoof. It was such a short name that she could easily do that. So she stretched out her hoof and scraped her name in the earth—Io, she wrote, and then Io again.

Her father looked to see what the heifer was doing, and as soon as he saw her name written there, he guessed what had happened. He embraced the heifer sadly, and when her sisters came running up, he told them the pretty animal was no other than their beautiful sister Io.

Now Argus had been watching and listening to all this. As soon as he learnt that the heifer was a nymph called Io, he sent the news to Juno. When she heard it she was very angry, and bade Argus watch the heifer all the more care-fully, for she felt certain that Jupiter would try to rescue her.

Jupiter, meanwhile, was very unhappy. He could not bear to think that the lovely nymph was a heifer, and he longed to change her back to her own form. But how could he outwit Argus of the hundred eyes?

At last he sent for Mercury, and bade him go and put the watchman to sleep, and then slay him. Mercury hastened to obey, taking with him a bunch of poppies. He dressed himself as a shepherd, and in the heat of noonday made his way to where Argus sat upon a high bank, from where he could see all the country round.

Argus was very dull. No one came near him, and he

He told merry tales to Argus

longed for company. When he saw the shepherd coming, he called out to him.

"Ho there, shepherd! Come and sit down on this bank with me!"

Mercury did so. Then he began to tell merry stories to Argus, and to sing him tuneful songs. But these kept the watchman more wide awake than ever. Not one of his hundred eyes closed.

Then Mercury began to tell him a long tale, dull and boring. Argus yawned, and closed two of his eyes. The sun was very hot, and everything was very quiet. Only Mercury's voice went on and on, like a murmuring stream.

Argus tried to listen, but he was too sleepy. Two more of his eyes closed, and then two more. He yawned more widely than ever, and when he had finished yawning, Mercury saw that ten of his eyes were now closed tightly.

The story-teller droned on and on. Argus closed more and more of his eyes, and at last lay back on the grass. Mercury bent over him, and saw that about twenty of his eyes were still wide open, keeping a watch on Io. He went on with his long, dull tale, often repeating himself, until he saw that ninety-eight of Argus's eyes were fast closed, and only two were open.

But these two were very bright and wide awake. No matter how hard Mercury tried, he could not get them to close. They shone steadily, following every movement of Io's.

Then, taking his bunch of poppies, Mercury shook them over the watchman's head. The magic in them caused Argus to be so full of sleep that even his last pair of eyes felt heavy and dull. He longed to close them, but for a long while he would not. Then at last Mercury saw them closing—Argus was fast asleep, and all his hundred eyes were shut.

Swiftly he slew the sleeping watchman. Then, taking the heifer's rope, he led her away to Jupiter, who gladly changed her back again to her right form. The poor maiden was overjoyed to be herself once more, but for a long time she did not dare to speak, being fearful lest she should bellow.

That evening Juno came to see Argus. When she found him lying dead, she was full of sorrow. She took his hundred eyes, and placed them in her peacock's tail, in memory of her faithful guard; and there they are to this day for every one to see.

The Story of Echo and Narcissus

ECHO was a lovely nymph, who was so fond of the sound of her own voice that she seldom stopped talking. One day she met the goddess Juno, and talked so much to her that she was rebuked for chattering. Echo answered the goddess rudely, and angered her.

"For punishment you shall lose your voice!" said Juno. "You shall never speak again except to repeat the last words of others! Go and hide yourself away among the hills, and do not dare to come forth and show yourself until some one bids you do so!"

Echo ran away in dismay. When she tried to speak she found that her voice was gone. It was only when she heard others talking that she could say anything—and even then she could say nothing but the last word she heard.

One day there came to the hills a beautiful youth called Narcissus. His body was straight and white, and his face was fairer than any nymph's. His black hair curled over his broad forehead, and his bright eyes sparkled and shone. Echo peeped from behind a tree and saw him.

At once she fell in love with him, and longed for him to love her. But how could she show herself to him, for Juno had forbidden her to come forth from her hiding-place unless some one bade her do so.

Echo followed the beautiful youth up the mountain. He heard a rustling noise behind him, and stopped. He looked round, but could see no one. On he went again—but soon stopped once more, certain that some one was following him.

"Who is there?" he cried.

Echo watched Narcissus from behind a tree

"There!" answered Echo, repeating his last word.
"Who are you?" asked the youth, seeing no one.
"You!" answered Echo.
"Do not mock me!" cried Narcissus angrily.
"Me!" said poor Echo.

"Come forth and show yourself here!" commanded Narcissus.

"Here!" Echo answered gladly, and stepped forth in all her loveliness. But Narcissus was angry. He was very vain, and thought that Echo had mocked him. He paid no heed to her loving looks, and when she put her arms round him, he pushed her roughly away.

"I heard you mocking me!" he said angrily. "Why do you pretend to love me? You are only making fun of me, and no doubt your friends are behind the trees, laughing. Go away!"

Sadly Echo obeyed him, murmuring "Away!" as she glided between the trees, wishing with all her heart that the proud youth might himself love in vain, and know what pain it was.

Narcissus went on his way up the mountain. Soon he felt thirsty, and coming to a clear pool, he lay down to drink from it. Suddenly he saw in the water the reflection of his own beautiful face—but he thought it was a nymph looking up at him from the pool, and straightway he fell in love with his own reflection.

"Sweet nymph, beautiful nymph, will you not come from your pool and play with me?" he begged. The lovely face in the water moved its lips as he moved his— but Narcissus could hear no sound coming from them. He stretched out his arms into the pool, but no sooner did they touch the surface of the water than the lovely face vanished.

He waited patiently until the water became smooth again, and then once more he leaned over. He smiled at the face below, and was overjoyed to see it smile back. He spoke again, and saw the lips move with his. But plead as he might, the nymph would not come from the pool.

Echo, seeing him talking to some one in the water, peeped over his shoulder to see who it might be. When she

Narcissus lay gazing into the pool

saw that there was only his own reflection there, she longed to tell him that he had fallen in love with himself. But she could not, for she could only repeat his last words. Then she became very sad, for she saw that her wish had come true—Narcissus loved in vain, for his reflection could never return the fondness he showed it.

The poor youth would not leave the pool. In vain he begged the nymph to come forth, in vain he smiled and stretched out his arms. All day long he lay there, and all night, for when the bright moon rode in the sky, he saw his reflection clearly, and spoke to it lovingly.

Days went by, and still Narcissus lay by the water. He neither ate nor drank, for he had forgotten everything save his love for the nymph in the pool. He wept tears into the water, but when he found that they sent away his reflection, and broke it up, he wept no more. He could not bear the nymph to go away.

Soon he grew thin and pale, and the nymph in the water did likewise. Narcissus was very unhappy. Echo too was miserable, for she knew that he would soon die—but she could say nothing to warn him.

One morning, when the sun rose, the beautiful youth lay pale and dead. So white he was and so lovely as he lay there by the pool, that the gods themselves wept for him and his hopeless love. In pity they changed his body into a flower as white and lovely as himself—the little narcissus that loves to grow by the side of water.

And still the flower bends over to look at itself in the pools, even as Narcissus leant over to gaze at his own reflection long years ago.

As for the poor nymph Echo, she pined away in sorrow, until there was nothing left of her but a voice. You may hear her still, among the hills, repeating your last words—but never again will she be seen.

The King with the Golden Touch

MIDAS, the richest king in the world, sat on his throne, thinking of his treasure-house. He longed to be richer still; he wished to have so much gold that no one could count it. But no matter how deeply he thought, he could find no way by which he might make himself still richer.

As he sat there thinking and planning, some shepherds came into the hall, and bowed low before the king. With them they brought an old man, Silenus.

"Lord," said the shepherds. "We found this old man wandering in your orchard. He is lost."

"It is Silenus, friend of the god Bacchus!" said Midas. He descended from his throne, and welcomed the old man. "You shall stay with me in my palace for ten days," he said. "I will feast you, and treat you well, and then I will take you back to your friend Bacchus."

So for ten days Silenus stayed with Midas and feasted royally. At the end of that time the king himself guided the old man back to the court of Bacchus.

The god was overjoyed to see his friend once more, for he had mourned him as lost. He embraced him, and then turned in gratitude to Midas.

"Ask what you will, and I will grant it," he promised.

Midas could hardly believe his ears. At last his chance had come! He could be richer than all the kings in the world put together!

"Grant that everything I touch shall be turned to gold!" he begged. "Let me have the Golden Touch!"

"So be it!" said Bacchus, laughing. "But do you think that will bring you happiness, Midas?"

Bacchus

"I know it will," answered the greedy king. "Oh, Bacchus, do you really grant this desire of mine?"

"The Golden Touch is yours!" said Bacchus, and turned to enter his palace.

Midas went homewards, followed by his wondering slaves. He longed to try his power, so he plucked a twig from a tree. Lo and behold! It turned to pure gold in his hands! Then the king knew that his wish had been granted, and he was beside himself with joy.

He touched his garments—they turned to glittering gold! But they felt very heavy, and the king could hardly walk. That did not trouble him, for he knew that they were now worth far more than before.

Then Midas stooped and kicked up some common pebbles on the path. As he touched them, they too turned to bright yellow gold. The king handed them to his gaping slaves and bade them carry them. Then he touched a clod of earth, which at once changed to the precious metal. In a short time the slaves were so heavily laden with golden objects that they could hardly walk along.

Soon Midas came back to his own palace. As he passed through the gardens, he plucked a red rose. To his great delight it became a perfect golden blossom. It had lost its beautiful fragrance and softness, but what did Midas care for that? Was it not gold?

He pulled apples from the trees, and threw them to his attendants to place in the treasure-house. He changed a whole tree to gold, by passing his hands over the trunk and branches. There it stood, bright yellow, very stiff and very ugly; but Midas thought it was the most beautiful tree he had ever seen.

He entered his palace, and threw himself down on a seat, tired with excitement. At once the seat became solid gold, too heavy to move.

He snatched at a cake

"Bring me water to wash with," commanded Midas. "And set the table with food, for I am hungry and would eat."

Slaves brought him a silver ewer of clear, cool water. Midas turned the silver into gold at a touch. Then he put his hands into the water.

At once it changed to gold ice! Midas could not wash his hands, and hastily he took them out of the curiously changed water. He sat down at the table, and saw with pleasure that the cloth, dishes, and glasses all turned to gold under his hands.

But now a great shock awaited the king. As soon as he put bread to his mouth, he found that that, too, turned to

Everything he touched was turned to gold

gold, and was uneatable! He snatched at a cake, and crammed it into his mouth quickly, hoping that he could swallow it before it became hard; but he could not. His teeth crunched on a golden cake, and he could neither bite nor swallow it.

The poor king took up a goblet of wine, and raised it to his mouth. He took a long draught, but even as it passed down his throat, it turned to a burning golden liquid, and Midas suddenly felt very ill.

He sat there, gazing at the fine food spread out before him, unable to eat a crumb. Soon his hunger overcame him again, and once more he tried to eat. The fish he took on his fork became stiff and golden, and the miserable king flung it down in dismay.

He arose, and went walking in the gardens, trying to forget his hunger. A slave approached him, but the king bade him go away, pushing him as he gave his command. At once the man became a golden statue, and stood stiffly on the grass unable to move or speak.

Midas was horrified, but he could not bring the man back to life again. As he stood there gazing in dismay at his golden slave, his children came running to him. Without thinking what he was doing, the king put his arms around them, only to find, to his great fear and horror, that they, like the slave, had all changed to little statues.

Then Midas was indeed unhappy. Could he, the richest man in the world, never eat or drink again? Were his beautiful children to remain golden statues? Was he to die of starvation, when by his magic power he could make enough gold to buy up all the corn, all the wine, in the world?

In despair, the wretched king fondled his golden children, and besought them to speak to him again, to look at him with their merry eyes. The little golden statues said never a word.

Then Midas ran through the gardens, and went all alone down the highway. He meant to go to the god Bacchus, and beg him to take away this dreadful Golden Touch. He walked as swiftly as he could, weighted down by his heavy golden garments, and at last, just as the sun was setting, he came to the court of the merry god Bacchus.

"Why do you return to me?" asked the god. "Have you not obtained the boon you asked?"

"Yes," answered Midas. "I have the Golden Touch, O Bacchus! But I come now to ask you to remove it from me, for I am very unhappy. I can neither eat nor drink, and my beloved children are changed to golden statues."

"Did I not say that no happiness could come from the Golden Touch?" demanded the god. "Keep your gift, Midas, and do not come whining to me."

Then the frightened king fell upon his knees, and with golden tears rolling down his cheeks, besought Bacchus to be merciful.

"I was wrong to love gold so much," he cried. "I am bitterly punished. Pardon me, Bacchus, and remove this hateful gift from me. What can I do to cure myself?"

Then the god was sorry for the unhappy king. "Go to the waters of the river Pactolus," he said. "Bathe yourself therein, and the Golden Touch will leave you."

Midas hardly waited to thank the god, but at once made his way to the river. He plunged into the cool waters, and saw that they became amber yellow. He felt the mysterious power leaving him, and rejoiced.

When he came out of the river, he found that the sandy bed had changed from silver to gold. To this day it has remained yellow, and even now men still pick up golden grains at the spot where the unhappy king bathed.

As soon as he came from the waters, Midas touched the twig of a tree. He gazed on it fearfully, dreading to see it

Midas filled the pitcher and ran to his palace

change to gold. But to his great joy it remained green and leafy.

"Now may Bacchus be praised!" he said. "The Golden Touch has indeed left me!"

He touched the ground, and picked up many stones, but they did not change. He plucked some ripening grapes from the hedge, and eagerly put them to his mouth. They remained soft and juicy, and with delight the king ate them, for he was very hungry.

Then he remembered his golden children and his golden slave. Tears sprang to his eyes, and rolled down his cheeks but this time they were real tears, not golden ones. He borrowed a pitcher from a nearby cottage and filled it with water from the river. Then he ran to his palace.

He emptied the water over his children and his slave. To his joy they came alive once more. The king embraced his children lovingly, and then, happy once again, turned to go with them into the palace.

He sat down at the table, and looked around.

"Take these gold dishes away," he commanded. "Bring me plain and common ones, for I sicken at the sight of gold."

In surprise his servants did his bidding. Then, taking his bread and meat from common dishes, the king ate the best meal he had ever tasted. The bread remained bread, the meat remained meat, and the wine remained wine.

Thus was Midas cured of his greed for gold, and learnt that riches do not bring a man happiness or peace.

The Story of Orpheus and Eurydice

ORPHEUS loved two things, his lute and the sweet maiden Eurydice. With his lute he made such wonderful music that everything listened in delight. All the wild animals left their lairs, and crept about his knee, the birds flew around his head, and the trees bent nearer to listen. Even the rocks softened when they heard Orpheus playing on his lute.

Eurydice loved his music too. When he came to woo her, she listened to his songs with joy. Soon she promised to marry him, and when the wedding-day came the woods rang with happiness and mirth.

But alas for Eurydice! As she danced at her bridal feast, she trod upon a snake in the grass. It struck at her in anger, and bit her foot. The maiden cried out in pain, and Orpheus ran to her.

But he could do nothing to help her. The snake was poisonous, and before night came, Eurydice was dead.

Then Orpheus was wild with grief. He went among the woods and hills, playing such mournful music on his lute that everything wept to hear him. He could not live without Eurydice, and at last he went to Jupiter, begging him to let him go down to the Underworld, where the gloomy King Pluto reigned.

"There I shall see my lovely Eurydice!" he said. "Let me go, O Jupiter, for life is nothing to me without her."

"Go then," said Jupiter, "but the way is strewn with perils, Orpheus. Think twice before you venture into Pluto's dread kingdom."

Orpheus turned to go, his heart lighter for the first time since Eurydice's death. He made his way to the black river Styx, and begged the ferryman, Charon, to ferry him across to the Underworld.

At first Charon would not, but when Orpheus began to play on his lute, he consented. Then, with sweet music in his ears, old Charon for the first time rowed a living man across the dark river.

Orpheus landed on the opposite shore. He went to the entrance of Pluto's kingdom, and there, lying by the mouth of the cave that led to the Underworld, was Cerberus, a fierce, three-headed monster. His duty it was to guard the entrance, and to see that nothing living passed in, and to forbid any dead spirit to pass out.

When he saw Orpheus, he made as if he would spring upon him and devour him. But the lute-player played such sad and enchanting music that the dreadful dog lay down and let him pass by in peace.

Through the caves Orpheus went, still playing on his lute. The spirits in the Underworld heard the sweet music, and came crowding round him to listen. Orpheus paid no heed to any of them. He had come to seek his beloved Eurydice, and her only did he desire.

Soon he passed by the wicked daughters of Danaus, who had killed their husbands on their wedding-night. For this they were punished by being forced to fill a bottomless cask. This they could not do, but if they paused for a moment a lash fell upon their shoulders, and they hurried to fetch more water. When they heard the lovely music of Orpheus, they rested in their hopeless task, and for a few moments tasted delight again.

Near by was the wicked King Tantalus. He stood up to his chin in pure, clear water, and over his head hung a luscious bunch of sweet grapes. The king was tormented by

Orpheus made wonderful music with his lute

a fearful hunger and thirst, but whenever he stooped to drink the water, if fled away from him, and if he put up his hand to the grapes, they swung out of his reach.

As Orpheus passed by, Tantalus for the first time forgot his hunger and thirst, and turned to listen to the lovely music. But Orpheus did not see him. Always he strained his eyes for Eurydice, striving to catch a glimpse of her sweet form among the shadows.

Soon the lute-player came to a steep hill, where the evil king Sisyphus was condemned to roll a great stone up to the top. But when he had just reached the summit the stone always slipped from his grasp, and rolled to the bottom. Then Sisyphus had to climb down and roll it up again.

When Orpheus came by, Sisyphus paused in his dismal task, and looked round in amazement to hear such sweet sounds in the Underworld. He sat down upon his stone, and for a little while forgot his woes in listening to the music. But Orpheus passed him without heeding. On and on he went until he came to the very throne of Pluto.

There sat the dark king, and by his side was the lovely Proserpina, her bright face shining out from the shadows.

"Why do you come here, mortal?" demanded Pluto. "Do you not know that only the dead pass through the portals of my kingdom?"

"O Pluto," sang Orpheus, "I come to find my sweet love Eurydice. Without her there is no life for me. You took her from me whilst she was too young—we had but just begun our happiness together. Give her back to me again, for I love her. Do you not remember, O Pluto, how you fetched Proserpina from the world above? Have you forgotten the love you felt for her then? I, in my turn, would fetch my love Eurydice from this world below. Oh, give her to me once again, or keep me here with you, for I will not live without her!"

As Pluto and Proserpina listened to the mournful song of Orpheus, tears sprang to their eyes. All the listening spirits sighed dolefully, and the air was full of soft groans. Proserpina leaned towards Pluto and whispered beseechingly to him.

Pluto nodded, and then turned to Orpheus.

Orpheus passed Cerberus

Orpheus turned to gaze at Eurydice

"Your wish is granted," he said. "Go back the way you came, mortal, and Eurydice shall follow behind you. But speak not on the way, nor pause. Do not look behind you, for if your eyes fall upon Eurydice before you reach the upper air, she will be lost to you for ever!"

Then Orpheus, a great gladness in his heart, turned away from Pluto's throne. He swept the strings of his lute, and the music that came forth from them was like laughter itself—a strange sound in that dismal kingdom. He passed upwards towards the faint glimmer of light that showed the entrance to the upper world.

Behind him he heard the following steps of his love Eurydice. He heard her soft breathing, and joy filled his heart. He spoke no word, and made no pause. On he went and on, and ever behind him came the patter of Eurydice's small feet.

Then, just as he came near the outlet to the world of sunshine and life, Orpheus wondered whether the time she had spent in the Underworld had changed Eurydice in any way. Would she look pale and wan, would some of her sweet beauty have fled?

Without thinking, the eager lover turned to gaze on the face of Eurydice—but no sooner had he turned than she sighed dolefully, and murmuring, "Farewell, a last farewell!" vanished from before his eyes. Down the long, dark passages she fled, and Orpheus stretched his arms out to the empty air.

Mad with grief, he tried to follow her, but he could not. He was led back to the world above, and there he wandered about with his lute, making such unhappy music that even the rocks wept to hear it.

At last he died, and then his spirit raced to meet Eurydice's. Gladly they embraced, and then, happy at last, wandered together in the lovely Elysian Fields, never more to be parted one from the other.

Clytie, the Sunflower Maiden

THERE was once a beautiful water-nymph called Clytie. She had wonderful golden hair, and every day she used to come forth from her pool, and comb it. It fell around her face in great waves, and shone in the sun like gold.

Clytie loved the warmth of the sun. She used to watch for Apollo's chariot to come through the gates of heaven every morning. Then the world was flooded with the sunrise, and hills and valleys rejoiced.

One day Clytie saw Apollo driving the sun-chariot. He wore his dazzling crown, and his face shone fair and bright. He was strong and handsome, and held the reins of his four fiery horses firmly in his powerful hand.

Through the sky he went all day long, driving the horses along the middle way. Clytie watched him, and admired his strength and his beauty. She was sorry when the sun-chariot entered the western seas, and was lost to her. Darkness came over the earth, and Clytie shivered. She returned to the water, and dreamed of the bright young sun-god all night long.

The next morning she arose before dawn, and stood by the side of the pool, watching for the return of Apollo. Soon a golden light tinged the eastern sky, and then the sun-god came forth once more. Clytie watched him eagerly. All day long she followed his course, sighing when he returned to the west.

The little nymph fell deeply in love with the handsome god. She thought of him and of nothing else. No longer did she return to her pool at night, but stood waiting in

Apollo looked straight before him

the darkness for the first golden gleam to appear in the
east.

She longed for Apollo to see her, and to return her love.
She felt certain that if he saw her waiting for him, he would
come to her with loving words. So all day long she watched
and waited for him to see her.

She combed out her pretty hair so that it hung round her
face like a sheet of gold. It gleamed in the sun, and shone so
brightly that her sister nymphs came up to her and stroked

Clytie had become a sunflower

her head. But Clytie paid no heed to them. Always she watched for the moment when Apollo would see her and smile.

But the sun-god did not turn his head. He looked straight before him, keeping his fiery horses on their difficult way. He did not see Clytie of the golden hair watching him with loving eyes.

Day after day the nymph saw Apollo drive out from the eastern sky, mount the heavens, and return to the western seas at night. Her face turned to him wherever he went, and followed his course all day long.

For nine days Clytie watched the sun-god, and never once did she take her eyes from him. She had no food and no drink, save only her own bitter tears. Then, on the ninth day, when she would have moved, she could not.

Her feet had become rooted to the ground. Her arms and fingers were green leaves. Her face, with its halo of golden hair, had become a flower!

Clytie was a sunflower. She could neither speak nor weep; but still she turned her golden head towards the sun, following his course the whole day through. And from that time to this all sunflowers do the same—their pretty golden faces look always towards the sun-god, as he drives his golden chariot through the sky.

The Story of Baucis and Philemon

ONCE upon a time Jupiter and his son Mercury came down to visit the earth. They dressed themselves as ordinary travellers, and went to the land of Phrygia, where they came one evening to a little village.

They were tired and hungry, and were glad to see the lights in the cottages.

"Let us ask for food and shelter here," said Jupiter. "We will see what kind of folks these be."

As soon as they reached the village, the children came out to see them. They shouted rudely at the strangers, and threw stones at them, while the dogs barked loudly, and made as if they would bite them.

Jupiter knocked at a cottage door, and when the woman came, he asked courteously if they might have food and shelter there. The woman laughed in his face, and answered him rudely that they had enough to do to keep themselves without feeding strangers. She slammed the door, and left the travellers standing on the doorstep.

At cottage after cottage the gods found the same answer. None would help them, none would give them even a drink of water. Jupiter grew angry, and vowed that he would bring destruction on such a wicked village.

Soon they came to a tiny cottage set a little way up the hill. It had but one room, but the garden round was neat, and the thatch on the roof was well patched. The gods knocked at the door, and it was opened by an old woman, Baucis.

Baucis and her husband, Philemon, had lived in the little cottage ever since they had first married. They had always been happy together, and, unlike the rest of the villagers, they were kind-hearted and courteous.

The villagers shouted rudely at the strangers

The old woman welcomed the two travellers and bade them enter. Philemon placed a bench for them, and put a cushion stuffed with seaweed upon it. Baucis went to the fireplace, and kindled a fire. She placed the little kettle on some sticks, and promised to give the strangers warm water to wash in, as soon as the kettle boiled.

Philemon went into the neat garden, and plucked some pot-herbs. He took down the flitch of bacon that hung from the roof, and cut off a piece. Baucis put it and the herbs into the pot. Then she poured some hot water into a wooden bowl, and set it before her guests, inviting them to wash.

Although the strangers looked like ordinary travellers, the old woman felt that there was something unusual about them. She wanted to give them the very best she had—but, alas, she had so little!

She took out a very old and coarse cloth to spread upon the table. It was snowy white, and was only used on special days. She set some olives on the table, and some berries pickled in vinegar. Philemon pulled some radishes from the garden, and brought cheese from the cupboard. Some eggs were cooked in the hot ashes, and served in earthen dishes. Then the stew from the pot was ready, and the two strangers fell upon the simple meal with good appetite.

At the end of the feast Baucis produced some ripe apples and some wild honey, beaming with delight to see how heartily her guests enjoyed their meal.

For drink there was some new wine in a pitcher. The strangers were very thirsty, and drank a great deal. Baucis began to feel astonished that her old pitcher held so much wine. The guests drank cup after cup, and yet the pitcher always seemed full. How could that be?

Baucis remembered they had an old goose

The travellers filled up their cups again, and drank. Baucis and Philemon thought that surely the pitcher must be empty now. They peeped in to see—and, lo and behold, it was full of wine to the brim.

Then the old couple were terrified, for they knew that their guests were no ordinary men. They looked at them closely, and knew them to be Jupiter and Mercury. Full of fear and dismay, they fell upon their knees, and begged their visitors to pardon them for the poor meal they had offered them.

"We gave you the best we had," they said, "but our best is very poor, we know. Forgive us, lords, for the coarse fare we set before you!"

Suddenly Baucis remembered that they had an old goose, who guarded their cottage for them. She would kill that as a sacrifice to the gods! She whispered to Philemon, and the two old people went out to get the goose.

But the bird did not wish to be caught and killed. It used its feet and wings well, and, hissing and cackling, ran this way and that to get away from Baucis and Philemon. At last it ran between the knees of the two gods themselves, and stayed there.

"Do not slay your goose, old people," said Jupiter gently. "We are gods, as you have guessed. We are grateful to you for offering us food and shelter, when you had so little yourself. You shall be rewarded, but all the rest of the village shall be punished. Ask any boon from us, and it shall be granted."

Baucis took Philemon aside, and for a few moments the good pair whispered together. Amazement and delight were on their wrinkled old faces. The gods were not angry, but pleased!

"Grant that we may serve the gods well till we die," said Philemon, "and grant, O great lords, that we may

each die at the same moment, so that one may not be left
to mourn the other. This is the boon we ask."

Jupiter smiled. He had expected Philemon to ask for

The old couple went panting up the hill

something magnificent—a palace, wealth, youth, perhaps—
but the old man's wish was so simple and small that the
god marvelled to hear it.

"Your wish shall be granted," he said. "Now come
with me to the top of the hill, for I would show you something."

The old couple went panting up the hill with Jupiter and
Mercury. When they reached the top, they saw a strange

Philemon's cottage had become a temple

sight. All the village was sinking into a lake, and every villager was drowned. Only their own tiny cottage was left standing, and even as they looked at it, it changed.

The corner-posts turned into great columns, the brown thatch became a golden roof, the earth floors changed to marble. The door grew larger, and became a beautiful portal, carved and adorned with gold.

"It is a temple!" cried Philemon, in amazement. "See, wife—our little cottage is a temple!"

"You shall look after it, and serve the gods there, as you wished," said Jupiter. "You shall be known as keepers of the temple, and when strangers come to worship, they shall hear your story."

Then the gods vanished. Baucis and Philemon went down to the temple, and entered it. They kept it to the end of their lives, living there happily and contentedly, welcoming strangers and telling them their story.

One day, as Philemon was standing on the steps relating the history of the temple, Baucis saw that a strange thing was happening. Philemon was putting forth leaves! She cried out in surprise, and Philemon turned to look at her. He saw that she too was putting forth leaves, and was changing into a tree.

"Farewell, dear wife," he said, and straightway a leafy crown grew above his hoary head, and he was a mighty oak. Baucis, too, was changed into the same kind of tree, and with their leaves they touched each other and whispered softly in the wind.

And still, so it is said, the shepherds show the trees to travellers, telling the strange tale of how they came to be there, so close together.

The Statue that Came to Life

PYGMALION, the King of Cyprus, was a sculptor. His clever fingers carved images of the gods and goddesses, and so beautiful were they that all men marvelled at them.

The sculptor would not marry. He did not like women, and vowed that he would never fall in love. Year after year went by, and still there was no queen to share his throne.

One day Pygmalion resolved to make the statue of a woman. Always he had carved and chiselled the likenesses of gods and goddesses, but now he wished to try his skill on the statue of an ordinary woman.

He set to work. Day after day he patiently wrought at a great piece of ivory, striving to bring the form of a beautiful woman from it. Soon the ivory took shape beneath his skilful fingers, and a wonderful statue stood in his workshop.

When it was finished, the sculptor looked long at it. He thought it beautiful—far more beautiful than the gods and goddesses he had wrought before. The face was very lovely, with the dawn of a smile on it. One hand was out-stretched as if to take his, and the sculptor took it, and caressed it.

"Oh, lovely statue!" he said, "if you were alive I would love you, and make you my Queen. Never have I seen a maiden like you before! You are beautiful beyond compare."

Every day the sculptor came to gaze upon his beloved statue. He called her Galatea, dressed her in fine garments, and crowned her with flowers. He placed a bracelet upon her outstretched wrist, and hung jewels round her slender neck. He was in love with this statue, but, alas! she could not love him in return.

Soon there came the feast of Venus, the goddess of love. Pygmalion went to her temple, and offered up a prayer.

Pygmalion offered up a prayer to Venus

"Great Queen of Love, hear me!" he said. "Grant that my beautiful statue may smile upon me! Grant that she may love me as I love her!"

Venus listened to his strange prayer. She heard what he said, and on her altar she sent up three tongues of flame. Pygmalion saw them, and felt his heart leap like the flames. Surely Venus would answer his prayer?

He went swiftly back to his workshop. There stood Galatea, his lovely statue, her hand outstretched as always. She was no woman, she was ivory, hard and cold. Pygmalion was bitterly disappointed. He had expected to find his statue alive, ready to welcome him lovingly.

He took the outstretched hand, and stroked it longingly. He looked into the beautiful face with its dawning smile— then his heart began to beat quickly, loudly—for surely the eyes were looking at him, surely the eyelids quivered, and the cheeks flushed red?

Then Pygmalion knew that his great wish was granted. His statue was coming to life! The eyes shone blue, the lips became crimson, and a shy smile spread over the lovely face. The hand he held became soft and warm, and trembled within his.

"Galatea! Galatea! Can you speak? Can you move?" asked the happy King. "Say but one word to me, I beseech you!"

"Pygmalion, my love!" said the living statue, and gave him her other hand. She stepped down from her pedestal beside the King, and he marvelled to see his statue walk with such grace. But she was no longer a statue; she was warm and living, soft and sweet.

In delight the King told her of his great love for her, whilst Galatea listened happily. And soon the two were wedded, and the lovely woman sat by his side, no longer a beautiful image of ivory, but a sweet and loving Queen.

The Story of Hyacinthus

THERE was once a fair youth called Hyacinthus, who was greatly loved by the god Apollo. The two friends went hunting and fishing together, and were seldom seen apart.

One day Apollo challenged Hyacinthus to a game of quoits, vowing that he would throw the iron discus at the mark, and would strike it easily.

The god took the quoit, and, with all his mighty strength, hurled it through the air. Just at that moment, Zephyrus, god of the south wind, came by. He too loved Hyacinthus, and was jealous because the youth liked Apollo best.

Seeing that Apollo hoped to hit the mark with his far-flung discus, the wind-god spitefully blew it aside. But, alas! when it fell to earth it struck the watching Hyacinthus, and smote him a fearful blow on the head.

The youth fell to the ground, wounded to death. Apollo ran to him in dismay, and took him into his arms. He tried to stanch the wound, but in vain. In a few moments the boy was dead.

"Oh, Hyacinthus, I have robbed you of your life!" said Apollo, in sorrow. "Never will I forget you, but in song and story I will tell your name, and your life-blood shall spring to beauty as a flower."

As the god spoke, the youth's blood dried up on the ground, and from it sprang beautiful flowers, which bore his name, hyacinth.

The god of the south wind, grieved to see that he had caused the death of the youth he loved, watched tenderly over the spot where the flowers grew, caressing them, and whispering to them endlessly.

Apollo took the wounded Hyacinthus in his arms

And every spring-time, when hyacinths blossom in the woods, the south wind visits them, murmuring to the listening flowers his sorrow for the jealousy of long ago.

The Story of Cupid and Psyche

THERE was once a king who had three daughters. The two eldest were very beautiful, but the youngest, Psyche, was so lovely that men could find no words to describe her. People came from far and near to see her, and whenever she walked abroad, flowers were thrown in her path for her little feet to tread upon.

"She must be Venus herself, the goddess of beauty and love!" cried those who watched her. "We will call her Venus, and we will worship her as a goddess!"

Now when Venus heard this, she was very angry.

"What!" she cried. "Is there a mortal girl who dares to think that her beauty compares with mine! I will punish her!"

She called her son Cupid to her, and he came, carrying with him his arrows of love.

"My son," she said, "there is a mortal maiden whom people worship for her beauty. Go to her to-night and slay her. Then those who worship her will know that she is mortal, and will be afraid."

Cupid filled a vase with some deadly poison and went to find Psyche. She lay asleep in her father's palace, her arm flung around her head. Cupid went to her, and was about to poison her when the moon suddenly shone out from behind a cloud, and lighted up the maiden's face.

Cupid stepped back in surprise, for never had he seen such a lovely maiden before. He dropped one of his own arrows upon his foot, and at once his heart became full of love for the sleeping girl.

He leaned over Psyche, and drank in her wonderful

Cupid dropped one of his arrows on his foot

beauty. He vowed that he would never hurt her, and when day dawned, he stole away as quietly as he had come.

In the morning Venus looked down to the palace to see if Psyche was dead. To her astonishment she saw her running in the gardens, playing happily with the pigeons there. Venus flew into a rage, and resolved to plague the poor girl and torment her in so many ways that she would no longer wish to live.

Day after day things happened to make Psyche miserable. There seemed no end to them, and at last the unhappy maiden vowed that she would end her life. She would

climb up to the top of a high mountain, and throw herself
down into the valley below.

She climbed wearily up to the top, and then threw herself over. But Cupid was watching her lovingly, angry
with his mother for tormenting the maiden so mercilessly.
As soon as he saw Psyche cast herself down, he called upon
Zephyrus, the South Wind, to catch her in his arms, and
bear her away to a distant isle.

Then Psyche found herself caught up in the soft arms of
the South Wind, and carried gently through the air to a
far-away island. Here she was laid gently down on a bank
of flowers.

She arose, and looked round her wonderingly. She found
herself in a beautiful garden, where thousands of fragrant
roses blossomed. Near at hand was a lovely palace. She
walked towards it, and as she came near, the doors swung
open to receive her.

Then gentle, unseen hands came about her, and soft
voices spoke in her ear.

"Welcome, lovely maiden!" said the voices. "Enter
and behold what is yours! Would you eat? You shall
find all you need, and all that you love best. Would you
sleep? You shall find a bed of down awaiting you, and
sweet music to play you to sleep."

Psyche was amazed and delighted. She entered the beautiful palace, and found a marvellous feast set ready for her.
Then she found a pretty bedroom, with a bed of down, as
the voices had said.

That night, when it was dark and his face could not be
seen, Cupid came to Psyche.

"Do not be frightened, beautiful maiden," he begged
her. "I love you, and I want you to be my wife. But you
must not see my face, nor seek to find out who I am, for
then our happiness would depart."

Psyche found herself in a beautiful garden

At first Psyche was frightened, but she soon lost her fear, for Cupid was so gentle and loving that she could not help but love him in return. All night long he stayed with her, and when he left she wept.

"I will return to-night," he promised. "Do not weep, pretty Psyche. I love you, and you are safe here in my beautiful palace. Everything you want you shall have, for I will grant all you wish."

Psyche smiled happily. Then she fell asleep till the golden sunshine flooded her room, and made it light. All day she ran in the garden, playing with the flowers and birds, longing for night to come when Cupid would return.

Each night the god of love came to his gentle wife and made her happy with his soft voice and many gifts. But never did she see his face, nor did she know who he was. She did not even wonder who he could be, for she was quite happy when she was with him—but soon she found the days so long without him that she sighed for company.

"Bring my sisters here to visit me," she begged Cupid. "I am lonely when you are not with me, and I would like to speak with them again."

"They will only bring you unhappiness," said Cupid. "Forget them, Psyche, and be happy by yourself."

But Psyche would not be happy until Cupid had promised to bring her sisters to her. So one morning the South Wind was sent to fetch them, and Psyche found them wandering in the palace garden, amazed to find themselves so suddenly brought from their home.

How pleased the lonely girl was to see them! She ran to them and kissed them, asking them a hundred questions. She led them to the palace and showed them all the marvels of it. She bade them seat themselves at the table, and then commanded her invisible servants to bring forth a wonderful feast.

Whilst they were eating, the two sisters asked Psyche how she had come to such a beautiful palace, and who had given it to her. They were astonished and jealous, for their own homes were poor and mean compared with their little sister's.

"My husband gave me this palace and all that is in it," said Psyche. "He grants my every wish, and is full of love for me."

"What is he like?" asked the sisters.

Psyche wondered what to say. She did not know what her husband looked like, for she had never seen him.

"He is kind and loving," she said at last.

"But what is his face like?" asked the sisters. "Is he young or old, handsome or ugly? And where is he? Why does he not come to greet us?"

Poor Psyche! She did not know what to answer. Her sisters saw that she blushed and looked down, and they knew that there must be something strange about their sister's husband.

They asked her so many questions about him, that at last Psyche confessed that she did not know what her husband was like, for she had never seen him.

"He comes when it is dark, and will not let me see his face," she said. "But I do not mind, for he is so kind and loving that I have no wish to know who he is."

"He is a monster!" cried one of the sisters. "Be sure he is an ugly monster, Psyche! Else why should he not let you see him, or know his name?"

"These monsters pretend to love you, and then one night they devour you!" said the other sister cruelly.

"Oh no, no, no!" wept Psyche, frightened and dismayed.

"You must be careful," said her sisters. "See, we will tell you what to do. To-night, get ready a lamp and a knife.

When your husband is asleep, light the lamp and gaze on him. If he is indeed a monster, slay him with your knife!"

"I will do as you bid me," said Psyche. "But now go, sisters. You have made me unhappy, and I would be alone."

The South Wind caught up the jealous sisters, and bore them back to their homes, leaving poor Psyche weeping bitterly.

"He must be a monster!" she thought. "Why should he not show me his face, or tell me his name, if he is not a monster? I must make ready the lamp and the knife."

She hid a lamp behind a curtain, and put a knife beside it. Then she waited tremblingly for her husband to come.

As soon as it was dark, Cupid came. He embraced Psyche lovingly, and kissed her soft hair. But she would not caress him in return, for she feared him to be a monster, as her sisters had said. Cupid was grieved to find her so silent, but soon he fell asleep, for he was very tired.

As soon as she heard him breathing regularly, and knew him to be sleeping, the frightened girl lighted her lamp, and took up her knife. She held the light over Cupid's face, and looked down on him, expecting to see some fearful monster, ugly beyond belief.

But what did she see? In amazement and delight Psyche gazed on her husband. Lying on the couch was a handsome youth, his head covered with golden curls, and from his shoulders sprang two snow-white wings. Psyche was so surprised that her hand trembled, and the lamp tilted.

A drop of burning oil fell on to the sleeping god's shoulder, and he awoke in pain. He gazed up at Psyche in astonishment and grief, looking on the knife in wonder.

He leapt from the couch, picked up his bow and arrows, and flew from the window.

"Farewell, farewell!" he cried. "I come no more!"

Psyche began to weep bitterly, reproaching herself for

thinking that her loving husband could have been a monster. She wished that she had trusted him—but it was too late. She had lost him.

Suddenly a furious wind began to blow, and the palace rocked to and fro. In terror, Psyche ran into the garden, and fell down in a faint.

When she opened her eyes again, the sun was high in the sky. The palace had disappeared, and where once the lovely garden had been, was now only a rocky wilderness.

Psyche rose to her feet, and looked around. She did not know where to go nor what to do. At last she began to walk westwards, longing to find her husband, and beg his forgiveness.

On and on she went, weeping and asking all she met if they had seen Cupid. But none could tell her anything of her lost husband. At last she met the goddess Ceres, who, remembering the great grief she had felt when she had lost her daughter Proserpina, was sorry for the weeping girl.

"Cupid is with his mother, the goddess Venus," she told Psyche. "He is ill of a fever, for his shoulder is burnt, and pains him very much."

Then Psyche wept more bitterly than ever, for she knew that it was she who had burnt his shoulder.

"What shall I do?" she asked. "Will Venus ever forgive me?"

"Go and ask her pardon," said Ceres. "She was once jealous of you because you are beautiful, and now she is angry because you have robbed her of her son, and have hurt him sorely."

So Psyche went to ask pardon of Venus. She knelt down before the angry goddess, and begged for forgiveness.

"Make me your servant," she said. "I will serve you well, great goddess."

Venus was very angry. She determined to set Psyche such difficult tasks that she would not be able to do them.

She led her to a great heap of barley, wheat, beans, peas, and millet.

"Sift all these seeds one from another," she said. "Have your task done by the sunset. Only by such labour as this will you earn your husband, foolish girl."

Poor Psyche! She knew that she could not sort out all the different seeds by the evening. She sat down in despair, and began to weep and wail.

A little ant heard her cries, and came running up. When he saw what was the matter, he went to fetch his many companions. All day long the little insects toiled for Psyche, carrying the different grains into different piles. When sunset came, the task was done.

Venus was greatly astonished.

"This is not done by *your* hands!" she cried wrathfully. She threw Psyche a crust of bread, and left her alone in the darkness.

The wild rams were as fierce as lions

Next day she came again, and showed Psyche a high hill, on the top of which a herd of wild sheep were feeding among the brambles.

"They are as fierce as lions," said the angry goddess. "I want a handful of their fleece. Go, fetch it for me."

Psyche climbed up the steep hill—but when she came near the rams, and saw them butting at one another fiercely, she was afraid. Then she heard a soft voice speaking to her from a nearby pool.

"Maiden, do not go near the rams whilst the sun is hot, for then they are fierce, and will kill you. Wait until the shadows fall upon the hillside, and then they will lie down in peace. You can then climb up to the brambles, and pluck the fragments of golden fleece they have left hanging here and there on the thorns."

So Psyche waited patiently till the shadows fell upon the hillside where the rams fought. Then they lay down peaceably, and the maiden was able to climb up and pick a handful of golden fleece from the thorns.

Venus was full of anger when she found that Psyche had been able to perform this task.

"So once again you have had help!" she mocked. "To-morrow I will give you a task in which no one can help you."

The next day Venus showed Psyche a strong black stream, that fell down a mountainside some way off.

"Take this crystal urn, climb up to the stream's source, and fill it for me, bringing it back before sunset," she commanded.

Psyche set off, carrying the urn. But as she climbed upwards, she saw that fierce dragons guarded the way, and her heart sank within her, for she knew she would be devoured. She fell to the ground in terror, and wondered what to do.

Then a great eagle saw her, and swooped downwards.

A great eagle saw Psyche and swooped downwards

"Foolish girl!" he screamed. "What do you here? Go back ere you are devoured. You cannot steal a single drop from the sacred spring, for the way is guarded too well."

Psyche looked at the eagle in despair. The great bird was touched by her sad face, and taking the urn from her hand, he flew upwards, carrying it in his beak.

"I will do your task for you," he said.

Presently he returned with the urn full of ice-cold water from the stream's source. Psyche took it gratefully, and the eagle flew away. Then, very carefully, the girl descended the mountain once more.

But Venus was still enraged with Psyche, and devised yet more difficult tasks, till the poor maiden became pale and worn with so much weary work. All this time Cupid was lying in his mother's palace, ill of his fever. But one day he flew from the window, hearing that the maiden he loved was being tormented once again by his mother.

Soon he found Psyche in a faint by the wayside, and she looked so pale and sad, that the god of love was full of pity and love for her. He kissed her tenderly, and she opened her eyes.

What joy was in her heart when she saw her beloved husband once more, and heard him speak loving words! Cupid bade her have no more fear, and took her with him to Olympus, the mountain of the gods. There he begged Jupiter to let his wife drink the nectar of the gods, which would make her a child of heaven like himself.

Jupiter consented, and Psyche was given a goblet of the wonderful nectar. She drank it and became immortal. Then a great wedding feast was held on Mount Olympus, and the two were united before all the gods.

Soon Psyche was taken once again to the wonderful palace, and there she lived in happiness with her husband, seeing him not only by night, but by day as well.

The Wings of Icarus

THERE was once a very clever man called Dædalus. Minos, the King of Crete, bade him make a labyrinth full of passages that turned here and there, crossed one another, and twisted and wound about in such a way that no one could find his way out, once he was in.

Dædalus made a marvellous maze, and the King was delighted with it; but before long a quarrel came between the two, and Minos shut Dædalus up in a tower. With him was his young son, Icarus.

For a long time Dædalus tried to escape, and at last he did so. But Crete was an island, and as soon as the King heard that his prisoner had gone from the tower, he set guards round the coast, with orders to search every ship before it sailed from Crete.

Dædalus knew this, and despaired of escaping from the island. But at last he bethought himself of the air.

"Minos may be king of land and sea," he said, "but he is not ruler of the air! I will escape on wings!"

He gathered together a great heap of soft feathers, and sorted them out into large and small. Then, beginning with the smallest, he stuck them tightly together with wax. When he came to the large ones he threaded them one to the other, and in this way made a marvellous pair of wings.

When they were finished, he fastened them to his shoulders, and, casting himself down from a height, was delighted to find that he could fly! He flew here and there, and then, satisfied that he really could fly, he floated down to his wondering son, Icarus.

"Make me some wings too," begged Icarus. "I will help you!"

The feathers floated down to the sea

The boy began to sort out the feathers for his father. Dædalus stuck them together with wax, and then threaded the larger ones just as he had done for his own wings. Soon a second pair was ready, and with trembling fingers Dædalus fastened them to his son's shoulders.

"You must practise first," he told him. "We cannot fly from this island over the sea to the distant land, unless you know how to manage your wings. Even the birds must learn to fly."

Icarus soon learnt how to manage his big feathery wings. In delight his father watched him flying here and there, up and down, like a great bird. When he saw that his boy could manage his wings wisely and cunningly, he made plans for their escape.

"We will start when the sun rises," he said, "for we must have all the day to see our way over the sea. Sleep well, Icarus, and rise early."

When the sun rose, Dædalus fastened on his own wings, and then strapped the second pair to his son's shoulders.

"Follow me," he said. "Do not fly too low, or the

spray from the sea will damp your wings, and clog the feathers. Do not fly too high, or the sun will melt the wax from your wings, and then you will fall. Fly along the middle way, and you will be safe."

So saying, he rose into the air, followed by the excited youth. High they flew, over the fields and hills, and shepherds and ploughmen cried out in amazement to see such a strange sight.

"See, there fly two gods!" cried the onlookers, and fell upon their knees in awe.

Soon Dædalus and Icarus left the island behind, and flew over the sea. Icarus was excited and happy, and soon, feeling safe on his big wings, he flew higher into the air. He was cold, and when the sun warmed him, he flew higher still, rejoicing in the heat.

But soon he flew too high, and the sun began to melt the wax that held the feathers together. They became loose and floated down to the sea. Icarus beat his arms up and down in fear—but his wings would no longer bear him. Down he fell, and down, and at last the sea swallowed him, and he was drowned.

Dædalus suddenly turned to see if his son was close behind. When he missed him, he called out in fear.

"Icarus! Icarus, my son, where are you?"

But there was no reply. In despair, Dædalus flew down to the waters, and there, floating lightly on the waves, were the feathers that had been in his son's two wings.

Then Dædalus knew that Icarus was drowned, and he lamented bitterly. He found the body of his son, and carried it to land, grieved that he alone should arrive alive and safe. In memory of Icarus, he called the waters the Icarian Sea, and to this day they bear the same name.

Arion and the Dolphin

ARION, the musician, lived at the Court of Periander, King of Corinth. He was a great favourite, for he could make such sweet music with his lyre, and sing such beautiful songs that every one loved and honoured him.

One day Arion heard that there was to be a great musical festival in Sicily. He went to King Periander and begged permission to take his lyre overseas with him, and try to win the prizes offered for the sweetest music.

"Do not go, Arion," said Periander. "Stay here with me, for I shall miss you sadly if you go far away. There is no music like yours."

But Arion begged so hard to go that at last Periander agreed. At once the musician set off for the far land of Sicily, taking only his lyre with him.

He easily won all the prizes offered, and was crowned the king of music. Then, laden with gold and jewels, he prepared to return to Corinth, eager to see his friend Periander, and to show him his treasures. He hired a ship to take him home, and prayed for fine weather.

The gods answered his prayer for a calm sea—but the voyage was not a fortunate one for Arion. The sailors on the ship caught sight of all the gold and the jewels that the singer had with him, and at once they began to plan to get it for themselves.

"We will kill him, and take his wealth," they said. "No one will know, for Corinth is far from Sicily. We will say that we have left him happy and famous in that distant land."

They went to Arion, and bade him make ready for death.

"Either we will slay you here, and bury you on shore, or you may cast yourself into the sea," they said.

"If it is my wealth that has turned you into pirates, take it for yourselves," said Arion. "But as for me, let me go, I pray you. Only give me my lyre—that is all the treasure I need."

The rough sailors laughed.

"You will have to die," they said. "If we take your wealth and set you free, you will tell King Periander what we have done, and we shall be punished. No, no, you must die. Choose quickly whether we shall slay you, or whether you shall cast yourself into the waves."

"I will throw myself into the sea," said Arion. "But first, grant me a boon. Let me dress myself in my loveliest garments, those which I wore when I was crowned king of music in Sicily, and let me sing one last song. Then I will do as you wish."

The pirates would not have granted such a wish, but Arion was so famous that they longed to hear his music; so they bade him garb himself as he wished, and sing to them.

The musician dressed himself in flowing robes of gold and purple, scented his long hair, and placed his golden wreath upon his head. In his left hand he held his lyre, and in his right the slender ivory wand with which he swept the strings. He strode to the side of the vessel, and, looking down on the deep blue waves, began his last song.

His voice was so beautiful, his song so lovely, and the sounds from his lyre so sweet that the listening sailors were entranced. Their hearts filled with pity, and almost they repented of their cruelty.

Arion played his last song to the sailors 9

When Arion had finished singing, he cast himself into the sea. The ship held steadily on her way, and soon the sailors forgot the pity they had felt, and joked as they divided his wealth between them.

Now, so sweet had been the singer's music that a herd of dolphins had been attracted to the ship. They had swum behind it, listening eagerly, enchanted by the delicious sounds that came on the breeze. When Arion threw himself into the water, they saw him, and came swimming round him.

The biggest dolphin of all knew Arion to be the maker of the sounds he had loved. He swam up to him, and offered his broad back to the struggling musician. Gladly Arion climbed upon it, and, holding his precious lyre safely out of the water, marvelled at his good fortune.

Swiftly the dolphin swam towards the nearest coast. Hour after hour he swam, whilst Arion composed a song in honour of his strange steed, singing it as he was borne along through the restless waves. Then at last land came in sight, and the dolphin parted from his rider on the shore.

Arion saw the towers of Corinth in the distance, and hastened towards them, singing as he went. He had forgotten his lost wealth, and was happy to think that he would soon see his friend Periander once again.

When he arrived at the court, the King took him in his arms and embraced him, delighted to see his musician back in safety.

"I come to you once more," said Arion. "But alas, Periander, I cannot show you the gold and the jewels that I gained in Sicily, for the pirates in my ship stole it all away. And I should have drowned, if it had not been for a kindly dolphin that brought me to land."

Periander listened in amazement as Arion told him all

The biggest dolphin swam up to Arion

his story. When he heard of the cruel sailors, he was very angry.

"I will punish them," he cried. "When they come to Corinth, I will command them to appear at court, and I will ask them what has become of you. You shall conceal yourself, and appear to them when the right time comes!"

The next day the ship sailed into the harbour. The King sent word for the sailors to come to his court, and very soon they arrived.

"Have you heard aught of the musician Arion?" asked Periander. "I am anxious for news of him."

"He is in the town of Tarentum, well, prosperous, and happy," answered the sailors untruthfully. "We left him there, lord, and he bade us tell you of his happiness."

At that moment Arion stepped forth from his hiding-place, and faced the amazed sailors. He was dressed in purple and gold, and on his head was a golden wreath. He looked exactly the same as when he had leapt into the sea.

The sailors fell flat on their faces in awe and terror. They felt certain that Arion must be a god, for had they not

D

seen him cast himself into the waters? And who but a
god could so marvellously appear before them, in the same
garb?

King Periander looked sternly upon the sailors, and they
trembled.

"Where is the wealth you took from Arion?" asked
the King. "Bring it here, and lay it at his feet. Then
prepare yourselves for death. Such a crime as yours can
have no other reward."

The sailors returned all the treasures they had stolen.
But when the King would have ordered them to be slain,
the musician stepped forward.

"Let them live," he said. "I do not want them to die.
Banish them to another land, O King. That will be
punishment enough."

So the wicked sailors took ship once more, and set sail
for distant lands, glad to have escaped with their lives.

The Boastful Spinner

THERE was once a fair maiden called Arachne, who was very clever with her loom and her needle. She wove such beautiful pictures that not only did men and women come to watch her, but even the nymphs left their woods and streams to see her quick fingers.

Arachne was vain. She thought that no one in the world could equal her in embroidering marvellous pictures. She loved to see the people standing behind her, wondering at her cleverness.

"Surely the great goddess Minerva must have taught this maiden her art," said the onlookers.

Arachne might well have been pleased to hear this, for the goddess was famous for her skill with the needle; but instead she was angry, and tossed her pretty head proudly.

"Minerva could teach me nothing!" she said. "If she came to me, she would learn many things, for I am better at weaving than she is!"

This proud boast of Arachne's came to the ears of the goddess. She arose and dressed herself as an old woman meaning to give the foolish maiden some good advice. Soon she stood by Arachne's side, watching the girl weaving a beautiful picture.

It was not long before the maiden began to boast again. She spoke lightly of Minerva and her skill, not knowing that the great goddess herself stood behind her.

"Put a guard upon your tongue, maiden," said Minerva. "Your proud words will come to the ears of the goddess, and she will punish you. Be warned in time, and beg her for forgiveness. She is merciful and will pardon you.

Minerva dressed herself as an old woman

Beautiful as your work is, it can easily be bettered by Minerva, and this you surely know yourself."

Arachne was very angry. She turned upon the old crone, and spoke rudely to her.

"Keep your advice until it is wanted," she said. "Tell it to your daughters or handmaids! I need no lessons from you, old woman! I tell you, I know what I am saying—Minerva could not do better work than I, and she knows it! If she thinks otherwise, why does she not come to try her skill with me?"

"She is here before you!" said the old dame. She suddenly threw off her long cloak, and stood upright in all her beauty and majesty.

The men and women, and the nearby nymphs, fell upon their knees and did her reverence. Only Arachne stood upright. She flushed a bright red, and then she paled. She was still defiant, and would not beg for mercy, or ask pardon for her bold words.

"Set up a new loom," commanded Minerva. "You shall try your skill with me as you wish. Choose a design, and I will do the same. We will set to work with our needles, and at the end the two pictures shall be judged."

Arachne set up her loom, and Minerva did the same. Then the two rivals took their needles and began to work. The goddess chose for her design a picture of the gods, with the great Jupiter in the midst. She put herself in the picture also, arrayed in all her glittering armour. The wondering onlookers saw her quick needle bring forth designs of wicked mortals being punished by the gods, of giants turned into great mountains, and of foolish girls changed into screaming birds.

Arachne worked swiftly. She was still proud and defiant, and meant to show the goddess that she was not afraid of her. Under her needle appeared pictures of the gods doing wrong and foolish things. The vain maiden hoped that she would bring a blush to the cheek of Minerva, when her rival looked upon her picture.

At last the designs were finished. The two weavers turned to see each other's work. At the first glance Arachne knew that she had been defeated. Minerva's picture was so marvellously wrought that it seemed to live.

The goddess gazed in anger upon Arachne's work. She saw that the girl had learnt nothing from her advice, or her contest—she was still vain and defiant. In rage, Minerva snatched up the embroidery and tore it to pieces. Then she turned to the frightened girl.

Before Arachne could run away, the goddess struck her. In an instant the maiden shrivelled up. All her hair fell off, and her eight fingers turned to legs. She was a spider!

The terrified watchers saw her run across the floor and hide herself in a dark corner, ashamed and miserable. There she began to weave a web, for Minerva still left her the power of making beautiful designs.

And from that day to this, Arachne's children have done nothing else. You can find their marvellous webs wherever you look.

TALES FROM THE ARABIAN NIGHTS

Where these Stories came from

DEAR CHILDREN,

Long ago there lived a Persian Sultan called Schahriah. He found that his wife had deceived him, so, in a fit of grief and anger, he killed her, vowing that he would take a new wife every evening, and cut off her head the next morning.

He kept his vow, much to the grief of the families whose daughters became his brides. Then one day the daughter of his vizier told her father that *she* wished to become the bride of the Sultan.

He was horrified, and reminded her that she would be killed the day after she had married him. She said that she had a plan whereby she might be permitted to live, and at last her father agreed to tell the Sultan she would wed him.

The Sultan consented to marry her, but said that, even though she was his vizier's daughter, she must die in the morning. That night he married her, and she went with him willingly to his palace.

She asked that her beloved sister might sleep near her, so that she could embrace her in the morning, before she died, and the Sultan gave his consent. Just before day-break the sister, acting on the bride's plan, came to her and begged her to tell her one of her wonderful tales before the time came for her to die. The Sultan gave his bride permission, and she therefore began her tale.

Now she was very clever at telling stories of all kinds.

She chose one that was most exciting, and the Sultan found himself listening eagerly. When the time came for her to die, the tale was not finished.

"You shall live till to-morrow morning," said the Sultan. "I wish you to finish the tale to-night."

But the tale was not finished that night, nor the next, for the clever girl always ended at such an exciting part that the Sultan could not bear to slay her until he knew what happened next. So she went on and on telling her tales, and every night the Sultan listened with enjoyment.

For a thousand and one nights his wife told him her marvellous stories, and at the end of that time he admired her so much, and loved her so fondly, that he could not think of killing her.

"I am ashamed of my vow," he said. "You shall not die, but shall live and reign with me."

In joy and delight the Sultaness threw herself at his feet and thanked him. She knew that she had not only saved herself from death, but also hundreds of maidens who might have been the one-night bride of the Sultan afterwards.

In this book are some of the stories she told. They are not split up or interrupted as they were when the Sultaness told them, but when you read them you can imagine the beautiful maiden reciting them to the Sultan, always breaking off at the most exciting part in order to continue them the next night, and so save her life.

The Rich Merchant and the Genie

THERE was once a very rich merchant, who had to go on a long journey. He mounted his horse, and rode off, taking with him a small bag in which he had put some biscuits and dates.

He soon arrived at his journey's end, and completed the business that had taken him such a long way from home. Then once more he took horse and rode off, eager to return to his family.

Three days he rode in the hot sun. On the fourth day he was so tired that he turned aside to rest under some trees. He sat beneath a great walnut tree, at whose foot ran a clear stream. From his bag he took some biscuits and dates, and began to eat, throwing the date-stones about him.

When he had finished his meal, he washed his face, hands, and feet, and said his prayers, for he was a good Mohammedan. He had hardly finished doing this, and was just about to rise from his knees, when he saw an astonishing sight.

Coming towards him was a giant-like genie with a long white beard and white hair. He was of a monstrous size, and held a scimitar in his hand. At the sight of him the merchant began to tremble with fear.

"Rise up!" said the genie, in a terrible voice. "I am going to kill you as you have killed my son!"

The merchant heard these words with amazement and fear.

"How can I have killed your son?" he asked, in a voice shaking with terror. "I do not know him, and I am certain I have never seen him."

"Did you not sit down here to eat dates?" asked the

The merchant begged the genie to spare his life

genie fiercely. "Did you not throw the stones about on all sides?"

"Yes, I did," answered the merchant, in wonder.

"Then you *did* kill my son," said the monstrous genie. "For he passed by here, and one of the stones struck him in the eye, and killed him forthwith. Therefore I shall kill you."

"Pardon me, my lord genie!" cried the merchant, in fright. "I did not see your son passing, and if I killed him, I did it unknowingly. Pardon me, I pray you, and allow me to live."

"I give no pardon," said the genie. "You shall die!"

He took the terrified merchant by the arm, and flung him down with his face to the ground, in order to cut off his head.

The man began to wail and beg for mercy so loudly that the genie did not at once let the scimitar fall, but listened.

"If you must have my life," said the poor man, "allow me to return to my wife and children and bid them good-bye. Give me a year, I beg of you, and at the end of that time I swear I will return here and you shall then do with me what you will."

"Do you take Heaven to witness your promise?" asked the genie, lowering his scimitar.

"Yes," answered the man. "I do. I will swear to come back here in twelve months' time."

At this the genie suddenly disappeared, and the merchant found himself alone. Hurriedly he mounted his horse and rode home. He told his wife and children of the dreadful thing that had happened to him, and they wept bitterly when they heard of his promise to the genie.

The year flew by quickly, and soon the time came for the merchant to return to the walnut tree where he had met the genie. With great sorrow he bade good-bye to his wife and children and set off. He came at last to the tree, and sat down under it to wait for the genie, trembling with fear and misery.

As he waited, he saw an old man coming, leading a deer. He was much astonished to see him in such a lonely place, and then was even more surprised to see yet another old man who was followed by two black dogs.

They greeted one another, and the two old men asked why the merchant sat sorrowfully in such a lonely place. He told them his story, and they listened in wonder.

"I shall stay here to see what the genie does," said the first old man.

"I shall do likewise," said the other.

Then suddenly all three saw a thick mist, like a cloud of dust blown by a whirlwind, coming towards them. It

An old man, leading a deer

disappeared, and out of its midst came the monstrous genie, his cruel scimitar in his hand. He came up to the merchant, and took him roughly by the arm.

"Get up," he said, fiercely. "I will kill you as you killed my son."

All three men began to wail and lament loudly. The old man with the deer threw himself at the genie's feet and kissed them.

"Lord, Lord," he said, "hearken to me. Let me tell you the story of my life, and of this deer by my side. If you think my tale is more wonderful than the adventure of this miserable merchant, I beg you to grant me one half of his body."

The genie looked at him, and stroked his long beard. Then, casting his eye on the deer, he answered, "Tell on, old man. I agree to your condition."

THE STORY OF THE OLD MAN AND THE DEER

Without delay, the old man began his story.

"This deer you see by my side," he said, "is my wife. We have been married for thirty years, and no children came to us. So at the end of twenty years I took into my family the son of a slave-woman, and brought him up as my own.

"This made my wife very jealous, although I did not know it, for she hid her hatred well. She waited patiently for a time to come when I should be away. This came when my son was ten years old, for I had to leave my family, and go on a long journey. So I went to my wife, and put the slave-woman and her son into her care, bidding her cherish them both until I came back.

"Whilst I was gone my wife began to learn the art of magic. As soon as she knew enough for her purpose, she changed my boy into a calf, and the slave-woman into a cow. She gave the calf to my farmer, bidding him fatten it up, and also the cow.

"When I returned, I asked to see the slave and her child.

" 'Your slave is dead,' said my wife. 'As for the boy, I cannot tell what has become of him. He has not been seen for two months.'

"This troubled me very much. I waited eight months for my son to return, but he did not. Then, the feast of

Bairam being near, I sent to my farmer for a fat cow to sacrifice at the festival.

"He sent me one. It was no other than the unfortunate slave-woman, whom my wife had changed into a cow. As I was about to kill her, she lowed pitifully, and I was amazed to see tears streaming from her eyes.

"'I cannot kill this cow,' I said to the farmer. 'Get me another.'

"My wife, who was standing near by, was angry when she heard this, and bade me not to be foolish.

"'Very well,' I said. 'The farmer shall kill her, for I cannot.'

"My farmer at once slew the cow, but when we skinned her, we found that, although she seemed so fat, she was nothing but bones.

"'Take her away,' I said to the farmer. 'Do with her what you will. She will not do for sacrifice. Bring me a fat calf instead.'

"The farmer went away, and soon returned, bringing with him a fine fat calf. I did not know that the animal was my son, yet I could not help loving the calf when I saw him. On his part, he grew excited as soon as he saw me, and tried to come to me. He broke his rope, and threw himself at my feet, doing his best to beg me to spare him, and to show me that he was my son.

"'I cannot sacrifice this calf,' I said. 'Take him away, farmer, and see that you care for him properly.'

"My wife was full of anger when she heard me say this, but I would not alter my mind. The calf listened with tears in his eyes. Then the farmer led him away.

"Next morning the man came to me, and said he wished to speak with me privately.

"'Lord,' he said. 'I come to tell you a strange thing. My daughter, who has some knowledge of magic, saw me

The child of the slave-woman

leading this calf away yesterday, as you bade me. She laughed and then cried, and when I demanded to know why, she told me truthfully.

" ' "My father," she said. "The calf you are leading is

no other than our master's son, and I laughed for joy to see that he had not been sacrificed. I wept soon after because I remembered how his mother, the cow, had been killed just before." '

" 'Can this be true?' I asked the farmer, in horror and amazement. I went at once to the shed where the calf stood. I embraced him, and knew that he was my boy.

"Then I sent for the farmer's daughter, and asked her if she could by magic restore my son to his proper shape.

" 'Yes, I can,' she answered. 'But only if you will grant that he may be my husband, and will allow me to punish the one who treated him so wickedly.'

"These conditions I agreed to, whereupon the girl took a vessel of water, and pronounced some strange words over it. She then threw it over the calf, who at once changed into my son.

"I ran to him, and embraced him with joy. The maiden married him, but before she did so, she punished my wife by turning her into the deer you see by my side.

"My son went travelling, and as I have not heard of him for some time, I am going in search of him. I could not trust my wife to any one whilst I was gone, so I have brought her with me, as you see. Now do you not think, O genie, that my story is even more wonderful than that of this miserable merchant at my side?"

"It is truly as you say," said the genie, who had listened marvelling to the tale. "I grant you half the man's body."

"Listen now to *my* tale," said the old man with the two black dogs. "If you think it more wonderful than the tale of the deer, pray grant me the other half of this merchant's body."

"Tell on," said the genie. So the old man began.

THE STORY OF THE OLD MAN AND THE TWO BLACK DOGS

"Great prince," he said, "these two black dogs you see are my brothers. When our father died he left us a thousand sequins each, and we all became merchants.

"My eldest brother soon sold his estate, and went travelling, intending to trade in far-off countries. At the end of a year a poor man came to my shop.

"I thought he had come to beg for money, and I greeted him.

" 'God keep you,' I said.

" 'And you also,' he said. 'Is it possible, brother, that you do not know me?'

"Then I saw, to my grief, that the poor man was none other than my unfortunate brother, who had lost all his money in his travels, and was now come back to beg help from me. As I had doubled my thousand sequins, I made haste to give him half.

"Soon after this my second brother sold his estate, and joined a caravan to go trading. But alas! At the end of a year he also returned, all his money gone. I had again made my thousand sequins into two, and willingly I gave him a thousand for himself, to make up his loss.

"Some time later my two brothers came to me, and besought me to go trading with them in a ship. For a long time I refused, but they pressed me so hard that at last I gave way. But when we came to buy the goods to take with us in the ship, I found that they had spent all the thousand sequins I had given to each of them, and had none left. So it fell to me to take my own money and spend that.

"I had six thousand sequins by now. I spent three

The old man with the black dogs

thousand of them in goods, and hid the other three in a corner of my house.

" 'For,' I said to my brothers, 'when you have gone trading before, you have lost all. If the same misfortune befalls us this time, we shall at least have a thousand sequins each, waiting for us at home.'

"Then we set off in our ship. After a month's sail we came to a port, where we landed. We sold our goods to much profit, mine especially.

"Just as we were about to embark again, I met a maiden on the seashore. She was very beautiful, but her dress was old and ragged. She greeted me, and much to my surprise begged me to marry her. I would not consent, but she kissed my hand, and prayed me so hard to take her with me, that at last I said I would.

"I bought her some fine dresses, and married her before embarking on my ship. As the days went on I found that she was as good as she was beautiful, and I loved her more and more.

"My two brothers began to be very jealous of me. They were angry because I had sold my goods at a better price than theirs, and they could not bear to see me so happy with my beautiful wife. So one night, when we were both asleep, they took us and threw us into the sea.

"Now, I should surely have been drowned if it had not been for my wife. I had hardly touched the water when she took me up, and bore me to an island. I was amazed, but when I heard what she had to say, I was even more surprised.

" 'I am a fairy,' she said. 'When I saw you about to embark on your ship, I fell in love with you. I disguised myself as a poor woman, to see if you would have pity on me. You were kind and generous, and I am glad to repay you for your good nature. But as for those two brothers of yours, I shall slay them!'

"I thanked the fairy for her goodness to me, but begged her not to have vengeance on my brothers.

" 'Pardon them,' I said. 'I do not wish their death, even though they have tried to drown me.'

"Then I told her all I had done for them—but when she heard, she flew into such a terrible rage that nothing would pacify her but to fly after them, and sink their ship.

" 'No, fair lady,' I said. 'Remember they are my brothers. We must return good for evil, so calm your anger.'

"Very soon the fairy transported me from the island to the roof of my house, and then disappeared. I went to the corner where my three thousand sequins were hidden, and took them. Then I made my way to my shop, which I opened, and began to trade as my custom was.

"When I returned to my house, I was surprised to see two black dogs there. They came up to me, and lay down at my feet. They tried in every way to show me that I was their master, and I could not think where they had come from.

"Then suddenly the fairy appeared again.

" 'Husband,' she said, 'do not be surprised at these two black dogs. They are your brothers.'

" 'My brothers!' I exclaimed. 'How came they to be changed into dogs?'

" 'I changed them,' she said. 'I flew after their ship and sank it. Then I turned your brothers into dogs, and brought them here. They shall remain for five years in this shape for a just punishment. At the end of that time, come to find me, and I will transform them into men again.'

"With that she vanished from my sight.

"The five years are now ended, so I am travelling in search of my fairy wife, taking with me my two brothers who, as you see, are still black dogs. Now, O lord genie, do you not think my story is even more marvellous than that of the old man with the deer?"

"Yes," said the genie. "I own it. Take your half of the merchant's body, and do what you will with it."

So saying, he disappeared utterly, to the great delight of all three men.

"Keep my half of your body for yourself!" said the old man with the deer.

"And mine also," said the old man with the two black dogs. "Thus you are saved from death, O merchant."

The grateful man thanked his two friends with tears in his eyes. Then he said good-bye to them, and each went on his way. The merchant returned home to his wife and children, and lived happily ever after.

The Fisherman and the King of the Black Isles

ONCE UPON a time there was an old fisherman, so poor that he had scarcely enough money to keep his wife and three children. Every day he went to fish in the sea. He cast his nets four times only, for it was his rule to do no more than that each day.

One morning, very early, when the moon still rode in the sky, he took his nets and went down to the sea. He cast them into the water, and then drew them towards the shore. He felt them to be very heavy, and he rejoiced, thinking he had a fine catch of fish.

But he soon found that he had caught nothing but the carcass of an ass. A second time he cast his nets, and again found them heavy. He drew them in, and discovered he had got a wicker basket full of stones and mud. In great disappointment he mended his torn net, and threw it into the water a third time.

Once more his net became heavy, but alas for the poor man! Stones, slime, and sand filled the meshes, and he was nearly mad with despair, for now he had but one more time to throw his net.

A fourth time he cast it, waited a little, and drew it in. It felt very heavy, and was difficult to drag to shore. The fisherman rejoiced, for he thought surely he had been lucky at last. He looked eagerly in the net, but saw no fish. Instead he found a big jar made of yellow copper, which seemed by its weight to be full of something.

The jar was tightly fastened and sealed with lead. The

fisherman took it out of the net, and looked at it with joy.

"I can sell this jar!" he said. "With the money I get I shall buy a measure of corn."

He looked at the seal on it, and wondered if anything precious was inside. He shook it, but could hear nothing rattle. He took out his knife, and broke the seal. Then he turned the jar upside down to see what would come out of it.

But to his surprise nothing came out at all. This puzzled the old man, for he could not think why it felt so heavy, or was so well sealed, if there was nothing inside. He turned it the right way up, and stood it on a rock, looking at it closely.

Suddenly a very thick smoke began to stream out of the mouth of the jar. The fisherman stepped back in astonishment, and watched it. It rose as high as the clouds, and spread all over the sea and the shore, making a great mist. The old man gaped at it, startled and amazed.

When all the smoke was out of the jar, it began to collect itself together, until it became a solid body. Then the fisherman saw that it had taken the shape of a genie, twice as big as the greatest of giants. He was so terrified that he tried to run away, but his legs would not carry him.

Then the genie spoke.

"Solomon, Solomon!" he cried. "Pardon me, I beseech you! I will henceforth obey you!"

The fisherman heard him in amaze.

"What is this you say?" he said. "Do you not know that Solomon has been dead for hundreds of years?"

"Speak to me more civilly!" answered the genie fiercely. "Or I will kill you."

"But what have I done that you should kill me?" asked the poor fisherman. "Have I not done you the great service of freeing you from your imprisonment in that jar?"

The smoke had taken the shape of a genie

"I shall kill you because of a vow I have made," answered the genie. "Listen to my story. King Solomon shut me up in the jar, because I would not obey him. He threw it into the deep sea, and there I remained for centuries. Now the first hundred years I was in the jar I vowed that whoever should free me should be rewarded by wealth. The second hundred years I vowed that my rescuer should have all the treasure of the earth. The third hundred years I promised that whoever freed me should become a powerful monarch, and that I would be his servant, and grant him three boons every day, no matter what they might be.

"But the centuries went by, and still I was a prisoner. Then I became angry, and vowed that whoever should free me should die straightway. You must therefore be killed."

The fisherman listened and trembled with fear. He begged for mercy, but the genie scorned his pleading. Then a cunning plan came into the poor man's mind.

"Before I die," he said, "I beg you to tell me one thing —were you really in that small jar?"

"You know that I was," answered the genie.

"I can hardly believe you," said the fisherman. "Why, not even one of your feet would go into the jar, so how could your whole body be there?"

"I swear to you that I was in that jar," said the genie angrily. "How can you say that you do not believe me?"

"I certainly shall doubt your word unless you show me that you truly *were* in the jar," said the fisherman. "It is impossible!"

At that the angry genie began to dissolve himself into smoke again, and soon streamed into the jar, until not even a wisp was left. Then a voice came out of the neck, saying:

"Well, now, unbelieving man, I am all in the jar. Do you still doubt what I say?"

The fisherman made no answer, but swiftly took the lid of the jar, and screwed it on tightly.

"Ha!" he cried in joy. "Now it is *your* turn to beg for mercy, genie! I shall throw the jar back into the deep sea again, and warn all poor fisherman against freeing you, should they catch the jar in their nets!"

The genie saw that he had been tricked, and besought the fisherman to free him again. He tried to get out of the jar, but he could not.

"Fisherman," he said, in kindly tones, "free me once more, and I will make you a rich man."

The fisherman longed to be wealthy, and he listened to the genie's promises. But he did not trust the monster, and refused to free him unless the genie swore to him in the great name of God that he would keep his word.

This the genie did, and since the fisherman felt certain that he would not dare to break such an oath as that, he took off the lid of the jar once more. Out came the smoke again, and soon the genie was there before the old man, who trembled a second time to see his huge form towering above him.

The first thing the genie did was to kick the jar right into the sea. He saw the look of fear that came into the fisherman's face, and laughed.

"Do not be afraid," he said. "I will keep my word to you. You shall be rich. Take up your nets, and follow me."

The old man did as he was bid. The genie led him past the town up to the top of a mountain. Then they climbed down to the plain, and after a time came to a great pond that lay between four hills.

"Cast your nets in this water," commanded the genie.

The fisherman did so, and caught four fish. They were curious creatures, for one was white, one yellow, one blue, and one red.

"Take these fish to the Sultan," said the genie. "He

The fishes in the pond

will give you gold for them. You may come here each day and cast your nets once, but no more."

With that he smote the ground with his foot. The earth opened, and the genie vanished utterly.

The fisherman, amazed at all his adventures, took up the four fishes, and made his way to the Sultan's palace. He presented them to the Sultan, who was delighted with them. He looked at them in wonder, and commanded that they should be cooked for his dinner.

Then he gave the fisherman four hundred pieces of gold, and bade him go. The old man, amazed at so much wealth, made his way home in a dream, planning what he should buy for his family.

The Sultan's cook-maid took the fish, and began to fry them. She put them into a frying-pan with oil, and when they were done on one side, she turned them over. But she had no sooner done this than the wall of the kitchen suddenly opened, and out came a maiden of marvellous beauty clad in shining satin, and arrayed with jewels.

She carried a stick of myrtle in her hand, and with this she struck the four fish.

"Fish, fish," she said, "do you do your duty?"

At first the fish answered nothing, so she struck them again, and questioned them. Then they lifted up their heads, and answered her.

"Yes, yes," they said. "If you reckon, we reckon. If you pay your debts, we pay ours. If you fly, we conquer, and are happy."

When she heard this, the maiden overturned the frying-pan, and entered the opening in the wall, which shut, and became just as it was before.

The cook-maid was very much frightened. She picked up the four fish, but saw that they were not fit to take to the Sultan. She began to weep and wail with fright.

Soon the vizier came to see why the fish were so long in cooking, and the weeping cook-maid told him what had happened. He listened in amazement, and ran to tell the Sultan.

"Send for the fisherman and bid him bring me four more such fish," commanded the Sultan. This was done, and the fisherman promised to bring them as soon as he could. He went to the pond, cast in his nets, and brought out four fish as before. He took them to the Sultan, who gave him another four hundred pieces of gold.

Then the Sultan shut himself up in his room with the vizier, and began to fry the fish. No sooner had he turned them on their other sides than the wall opened, and out came a monstrous black slave with a green wand in his hand. He went to the fish and struck them, asking them, in a terrible voice, if they were doing their duty.

They answered as before. The slave upset the pan on the floor, entered the hole in the wall, and disappeared.

"This is a most amazing thing," said the Sultan, greatly astonished. "I am determined to know all that lies behind these strange fish. Send for the fisherman again."

Once more the old man came to the palace. The Sultan commanded him to show the way to the pond from which he took the fish, and the fisherman obeyed.

All the Sultan's court went with him, and were much amazed when they saw the pond lying between the four hills.

"This is strange," said the vizier. "For sixty years I have hunted in the land round about, but never before have I seen this pond, nor these hills."

The Sultan saw that the pond was full of the many-coloured fish, and he wondered how the water came to be there with all the strange fish in it. He called his vizier to him, and spoke with him.

"I have a mind to solve this mystery," he said. "I may be away some days, so do not be alarmed."

He put on a strong suit, took his scimitar in his hand, and when night came, left the pond and walked towards one of the four hills. He climbed it, and found a plain beyond. When the sun rose he was down on the plain, and saw some distance away a great building.

He found that it was a strong castle of black marble, highly polished, and covered with fine steel as bright as a mirror. He went to the gates, and knocked loudly many times; but no one came.

"This is strange," said the Sultan. "Well, I will enter. If no one is within, I have nothing to fear. If some one is there, I have my scimitar with which to defend myself."

He entered the gates, and, coming to the door of the castle, cried out in a loud voice, saying that a stranger begged for food. No one came forward to receive him, so he went through the door into the castle.

There were great halls there, furnished richly with tapestries and silken hangings, and embroidered in silver and gold. Every apartment was grand and magnificent. The outer ones looked out on marvellous gardens where were fountains, flowers, and trees, among which flew wonderful singing birds.

The Sultan sat down on a veranda, and looked out with pleasure on this beautiful garden. Suddenly he heard a sound of weeping and wailing, and grief-stricken cries came to his ears. He listened in wonder.

"Oh Fortune!" wailed the voice, "I am the most unhappy man in the world. Let me no longer live, but grant me a speedy death!"

The Sultan leapt to his feet, and went to a door hung with a silken curtain. He drew it aside, and saw a large room, at the end of which sat a richly-dressed young man on a throne. It was he who was lamenting so bitterly.

The Sultan approached him and bowed. The young man looked at him sorrowfully.

"My lord," he said, "I wish I could return your greeting, and rise to welcome you. But alas! I cannot!"

"That is nothing," said the Sultan. "Now tell me, I pray you, the reason for your cries. Can I not help you? And what is the meaning of the pond where the many-coloured fishes are, and of this lonely castle, and, last of all, why are you here all alone?"

The young man did not answer these questions. Instead he began to weep bitterly, and raised up his robe. Then the amazed Sultan saw that the prince was a man only to his waist, for from there to his feet he was changed into black marble.

He started back in horror, and bade the young man tell him all his tale.

"Listen then," said the prince mournfully, "and I will tell you a strange story."

THE HISTORY OF THE YOUNG KING OF THE BLACK ISLES

"This is the kingdom of the Black Isles, which takes its name from those four little hills, which were once islands. Its capital stood where you now see the great pond.

"My father ruled over this kingdom till his death. I then came to the throne, and married a beautiful maiden, my cousin. For five years we lived happily, and then I found that she no longer loved me.

"One day I felt sleepy after dinner, and laid myself down to rest. Two of my wife's ladies came and sat down by me, one at my head, and one at my feet, to keep the flies away with their fans. They thought I was fast asleep, and began to talk to one another in whispers.

From his waist to his feet he was changed into black marble

" 'How can the Queen not love such a kind prince as this?' said one.

" 'It is very strange,' replied the other. 'I know that she goes out every night, and leaves him alone. How is it that he does not notice this?'

" 'She makes sure that he does not!' said the first lady. 'She puts a certain herb in his evening drink, which causes him to sleep soundly all night through. Therefore he does not know when she leaves him or where she goes. When day dawns she returns, and by placing some scent beneath his nose, she awakes him.'

"I listened in astonishment and dismay. I pretended to awake from sleep, and the ladies ceased their talk. Then my wife came in, and we supped together.

"She mixed me my evening drink, but this time I did not drink it. Instead I went to an open window, and emptied the cup outside. Then I put it into her hands, and she thought I had drunk the potion.

"That night, when she judged me to be sound asleep, she arose and dressed herself.

" 'Sleep, and may you never wake again!' she hissed, for she had no idea that I was awake. Then she went swiftly from the room.

"At once I arose, took my scimitar, and followed her quickly. She went through several gates, each of which opened before her silently when she spoke some magic words. Last of all she passed through the garden gate, and then entered a little wood guarded by a thick hedge. I followed, and hid myself.

"I saw that she had met a man, and was speaking words of love to him. She offered to turn the city and palace into ruins, to show him how strong was her love for him. At this I was enraged, and, darting from my hiding-place, I struck at him with my scimitar, wounding him to death.

"Then, before the Queen knew who I was, I swiftly returned to the palace, and laid myself down in bed again. She ran to the help of her lover, and by her enchantments succeeded in keeping death away. But although he was alive, he could not move nor speak, so that he seemed more dead than living.

"I fell asleep, and when I awoke the Queen was at my side. She had dressed herself in mourning, and her hair was hanging about her eyes.

" 'Sir, do not be surprised at my sad appearance,' she said. 'I have had sorrowful news to-day. The Queen, my mother, is dead. My father the King has been killed in battle, and my brother has fallen into a river, and is drowned.'

"I pretended to believe her story, though I very well knew why she was so distressed. She mourned for a whole year, and then came to me with a request.

" 'Allow me to build myself a tomb in the palace grounds,' she begged. 'There I will remain to the end of my days.'

"I gave my consent, and she built herself a stately palace, and called it the Palace of Tears. She commanded that her half-dead lover should be taken there, and this was done. Every day she took him the magic potion which kept him alive, but no matter what she did she could not make him any better.

"He could not walk, speak, or move, but could only look at her. The Queen made him two long visits every day, and though I pretended to know nothing of this, I was aware of everything that passed.

"One day I went to the Palace of Tears myself. I hid behind a curtain, and heard the Queen speak loving words to her gallant, beseeching him to answer her. She wept and groaned until I lost all patience, and rushed out from behind the curtain.

" 'Wicked woman,' I said, 'cease your sighing and groaning. I should have killed you when I struck down this wretch.'

"I raised my scimitar, but she regarded me with a jeering smile.

" 'Stay your anger,' she said. Then she immediately chanted some magic words which I did not understand.

" 'And now, by virtue of my enchantments,' she added, 'I command you to become half marble and half man!'

E

"At once I became what you now see me—half man, half marble, neither living nor yet dead.

"The enchantress brought me to this hall and placed me here. Then by her fearful magic she destroyed my capital city, with all its houses, shops, and fine buildings, and turned it into the pond you saw. The people she changed into fishes. The white are the Mohammedans, the red are the Persians, who are worshippers of fire; the

The Queen ran to the help of her lover

blue are Christians and the yellow are Jews. To add to my sorrow, this wicked woman comes every day and lashes my naked back a hundred times with a whip."

The young King began to weep bitterly as he came to the end of his strange story, and the Sultan was so grieved that he could not say one word to comfort him.

"I will revenge you," he said at last. "Be of good cheer, Prince, for I will think of a plan whereby you shall be delivered from your unhappiness."

Then, as night was come, the Sultan lay down to rest, but the poor Prince did not sleep, for he had been unable to do so ever since his enchantment.

Before dawn came the Sultan arose, and made his way to the Palace of Tears. He found it lighted with many torches, and scented with delicious perfumes. On the bed lay the half-dead magician of whom the Queen was so fond. The Sultan put the poor wretch out of his misery and threw his body down a well in the courtyard.

Then he went and lay down in the bed, putting his scimitar under the counterpane, and waited for the Queen to come.

After the enchantress had given her miserable husband a hundred lashes with her whip, she entered the Palace of Tears, and leaned over the bed.

"Alas, my love!" she groaned. "Will you never speak to me again? How I long to hear your voice once more!"

The Sultan pretended to awaken from a long sleep, and spoke a few words in a low and feeble voice. The Queen heard him, and cried out in rapture:

"My dear lord!" she cried, "do I really hear your voice? Speak to me again, I pray you!"

"Wretched woman," answered the Sultan, "you are not worthy to be spoken to!"

The Queen began to weep.

"Why do you speak to me so reproachfully?" she asked. "What have I done to make you angry?"

"Do you not know that the cries and wails of your husband have hindered me from being cured?" said the wily Sultan. "Unless you restore the King to well-being, I shall never be able to speak to you again."

The Queen immediately ran out of the Palace of Tears. She took a cup of water, and said some magic words over it, whereupon it began to boil furiously. She then went to her poor husband, and threw it over him.

"Change back to your natural form!" she commanded. At once the Prince felt the enchantment leave him, and he saw that he was now a man from his head to his heels, and no longer half marble. He arose up in the greatest joy.

"Go!" said the Queen fiercely, "and never return to this castle again, or I will slay you!"

The young man at once went to a place some distance away, and there awaited the coming of the Sultan. Meanwhile the Queen returned to the Palace of Tears, and spoke fondly to the Sultan, thinking that he was her lover.

"Dear lord," she said, "I have done your bidding."

"You have not done enough," said the Sultan. "Do you not know that at midnight all the fishes in the pond raise their heads, and cry out for vengeance against me and you? Transform the pond back into the city it once was, and change the fishes into people. Then and then only can I be cured. When you have done this, come to me, and you shall give me your hand, and help me to arise."

Full of joy to hear this, the Queen hastened to do what she was commanded. She ran to the pond, and taking a little water in her hand, sprinkled it around, at the same time pronouncing magic words over the fishes and the pond.

In a trice a wonderful change took place. The pond became the great city it once was, and all the fishes were restored to their proper shape, and became people. In fact, everything became as it had been before the enchantment.

The Sultan's court, which had been encamped on the edge of the pond, were amazed to find the water disappear, and a great city spring up around them. They gazed about in wonder, and marvelled loudly.

The enchantress returned swiftly to the Palace of Tears.

"My lord!" she cried, "your commands are all fulfilled. Give me your hand."

"Come near me," said the Sultan.

She approached him. He arose suddenly from the bed, and with one blow of his scimitar struck the wicked Queen dead. Then he hastened to find the young King.

"Prince!" he said, "rejoice and fear no more. Your enemy is dead!"

The young man could not find enough words with which to thank the brave Sultan.

"Say no more," begged the Sultan. "You may now rule happily in your own land, or, if you wish, you may accompany me to mine, which is not far away, and where you will be much welcomed."

"Great lord," said the young King, "you are mistaken in thinking that your land is but a few hours away. It may have been, when my own kingdom was enchanted, but now that it is restored to its own place and form, it is at least a year's journey away!"

This the astonished Sultan found to be true. He was sad to think that he would be so far from the young man when he returned to his own land, and he begged him to accompany him, and to be his son.

"For," said he, "I have no child of my own, and if you will come with me, you shall be king after me."

This the young man agreed to, for he felt the greatest love for his deliverer. His cousin was made King of the Black Isles in his stead, and he himself went with the Sultan on the long year's journey.

When they arrived, the people of the Sultan's kingdom gave them a great welcome, and for many days there was feasting and merry-making. The Sultan took the young King for his son, and each of them was happy in the other.

As for the old fisherman, whose finding of the copper jar had caused such strange adventures, he was greatly rewarded. The Sultan gave him a fine estate, and there he and his family lived happily to the end of their lives.

The Story of Sindbad the Sailor

THE STRANGE LITTLE ISLAND

L ET ME tell you my story. I am Sindbad, a sailor whose adventures will fill you with amazement, for each of the seven voyages I have taken have been full of marvels of many kinds.

My father died when I was young, and left me much wealth. Most of this I spent foolishly. Then, when I was almost in poverty, I took the advice of some friends and went to sea. I took with me some goods which I hoped to sell at a profit when we touched at a port.

I embarked at Balsora, a port on the Persian Gulf. We set sail, and in due course arrived at several islands where we sold or exchanged our goods. Then one day the wind dropped, and we lay becalmed near a little island which was almost level with the surface of the water. It looked like a smooth, green meadow, and some of us resolved to land upon it, and stretch our legs.

We had not been on the curious little island very long before it suddenly began to quake and tremble. Those on board the ship saw this, and shouted to us to beware—for we were on no island, but on the back of a huge whale!

Some jumped into the boat near by, and others swam to the ship. When the whale suddenly dived, I was the only person left on its back.

I had time to catch hold of a piece of driftwood, and then had to struggle for my life. The captain took up those who were in the boat, and rescued those who were swimming, but did not see me. A favourable wind sprang up

I was stranded on the back of a huge whale!

at that moment, and I saw, to my great horror, all the sails of my ship hoisted. Then the ship drove off before the wind, and I was left in the sea alone.

I struggled in the water for a day and a night, and should certainly have been drowned if a big wave had not taken me and thrown me on an island. I lay on the shore half dead, and waited for the sun to rise and warm me.

When I had a little recovered, I went to seek food and water. I found some herbs to eat, and a spring of clear, cool water. Then, to my surprise, I came across a beautiful horse tied to a post.

It was a fine mare, and as I approached I was astonished to hear a voice calling me from under the ground. I turned and saw a man coming from a cave. He asked who I was, and how I came there, and I told him of my adventure.

He took me into the cave, where I found more men. I asked them who they were, and they told me.

"We are the grooms of King Mihrage," they said. "Every year we bring his mares to this part of the island. To-morrow we return, so if we had not found you to-day, you would surely have perished, for no one lives in this spot."

The next day they took me with them to the city where King Mihrage dwelt. They presented me to him, and he asked me all my story, which I told him truthfully.

"You shall stay here in safety," he said. "I will command that you want for nothing."

He was as good as his word. I was well looked after, and had everything I needed.

When merchants came to the town I went to talk with them, hoping to hear news of my own city of Bagdad, or to find some way of going back there; for the city of King Mihrage is on the sea, and has a fine port, to which come vessels from all parts of the world.

One day, when I was at the port, a ship arrived. The merchants on board commanded that the bales of goods should be carried ashore. I watched them, and looked for the name on each. Judge of my astonishment when I saw my own name, Sindbad, on some of them, and knew them to be the very goods I had embarked at Balsora!

I looked at the captain, and knew him. But as I felt certain he thought I was drowned, I asked him whose bales these were.

"They belonged to a merchant called Sindbad, who was unhappily drowned," he replied. "I am now going to sell them, and give the money to his family."

"Captain," said I, "those bales belong to me, for I am that Sindbad whom you thought to be drowned."

"What impudence is this!" cried the captain. "With my own eyes I saw Sindbad drawn under the waves."

"Patience, patience," I said. "Hear my tale, and then judge whether or no I am Sindbad."

Whereupon I told him all my adventures. He listened in amazement, and called some of the passengers of his ship. They knew me, and embraced me with joy and wonder.

Then the captain himself remembered me, and embraced me gladly.

"Heaven be praised for your lucky escape!" he said. "Here are all your goods. Take and do with them what you wish."

I saw a beautiful horse, tied to a post

I went to King Mihrage, and told him of my good fortune. I gave him a valuable present from my goods, bade him farewell, and embarked once more on my ship. We set sail, and went off before the wind.

By the time I once more reached the port of Balsora, I had sold my goods to such profit that I had a hundred thousand sequins to my name. My family were overjoyed to see me, and embraced me tenderly.

Then I bought many slaves, and built myself a great house. Here I settled down, eager to enjoy the pleasures of life, and to forget what I had suffered.

THE GIANT ROC AND THE VALLEY OF DIAMONDS

For some time I led a quiet and peaceful life. But soon I tired of this, and longed to go to sea again. I bought some goods, embarked on another ship, and began my second voyage.

We touched island after island, and sold our goods to

When I awoke, the ship had sailed

great profit. Then one day we came to an isle where grew
many fine fruit trees, but as far as we could see, there were
no people there at all.

We landed, and began to roam about. I sat down by a
stream, and soon fell fast asleep.

When I awoke, the ship was gone! I got up and looked
about for the men who had been with me on the island,
but could see them nowhere. Then, far on the sky-line,
I saw the ship, and soon she had disappeared altogether.

I thought I should die of dismay and sorrow. I beat my
head and breast, and cried out in despair. Then I bethought
myself to climb a tree, and see from there if I was near any
town.

On the sea side was nothing but sea and sky, but on the
land side I saw something white, though I could not tell what
it was. I climbed down, and made my way towards this.

When I came near I thought it must be a great bowl of
some sort, very high and very big. I touched it, and found
it smooth. I walked round it, but there was no opening
anywhere. It was at least fifty paces round. I could not
think what it might be.

Then suddenly the sky seemed to grow dark. I looked
up and saw a monstrous bird flying towards me. It flew
down to the ground, and sat upon the great white thing—
which I at once knew to be its egg!

I knew then that the bird must be a gigantic roc, of
which I had heard mariners tell many tales. A plan came to
me, and I swiftly unwrapped the folds of my turban. With
it I tied myself tightly to the great bird's legs, which seemed
to me like the trunks of trees, and waited for it to fly away.
I thought that then I should be taken from this barren place.

Next morning the bird flew of, taking me with her.
She flew very high, and I could not see the earth. Then
she began to fly downwards at such a terrible pace that I

fainted. When I opened my eyes again, I found myself on the ground with the great roc. I at once untied myself, and no sooner had I done so than the bird rose into the air again, having in her beak an enormous serpent.

I looked round and saw that I was in a deep valley. It was surrounded by such high, steep mountains that I saw at once I could not climb them. How then was I to get out? I seemed to be even worse off than when I was on the desert island.

As I walked about I saw that diamonds were strewn over the ground. Some of these were so enormous that I looked on them with delight. But I soon saw something that took all my pleasure away—for in the distance were serpents, huger than any I had ever seen or heard of. Even the smallest of them could have swallowed an elephant!

I walked about all day, and when night drew near I found a small cave where I thought I should be safe from the snakes. I went inside, and shut up the mouth of it with a large stone. It did not quite close the cave, but allowed a little daylight to enter. When it was quite dark I lay down to sleep.

But the serpents came all round my cave, and I could hear them hissing in a fearful manner. I was so afraid that I could not even close my eyes. I was glad when daylight entered the cave, and the snakes glided away. They feared the giant rocs, and went to hide themselves.

Trembling, I pushed the stone away, and went out into the valley once more. I had passed such a terrible night that I walked on the diamonds without giving them a thought. Then, as I was very tired and sleepy, I sat down, and thought I would sleep for a while.

I had no sooner shut my eyes than I was awakened by something rolling by me with a great noise. I jumped to my feet, and saw to my surprise that a large piece of fresh meat had rolled by me. As I looked at it in amazement, I saw several other pieces coming down from the rocks in the mountains.

Then I knew that I was in the famous Valley of Diamonds which had never been trodden by the foot of man, owing to the steep mountains that protect it. I knew also the meaning of the pieces of meat, for I had many times heard

The merchants accused me of stealing their diamonds

of the trick that merchants used in order to get diamonds from this valley.

There are many eagles in this country, and in the season when they nest and have young ones, the merchants throw large joints of meat into the Valley of Diamonds. These roll over many precious stones, which stick to them. The eagles pounce on the meat and carry it away in their claws to their nests. The merchants run to the nests, frighten away the eagles, and then take the diamonds out of the meat. Thus do they enrich themselves.

Up till that moment I had thought that never should I be able to get out of this valley; but when I saw the meat rolling by me, an idea came into my mind, and I rejoiced. I swiftly gather up the biggest diamonds I could see, and filled my wallet with them. Then I went to the largest piece of meat in the valley, and tied myself to it with the long rolls of my turban.

I lay face downwards, waiting for the coming of the eagles. Soon I felt one pick me up in its strong claw, and bear me away to the mountain-top. As soon as it had placed me in its nest, the merchants began shouting to frighten it away. Then they ran to see if there were any diamonds in the meat.

When they saw me, they were very much alarmed, but soon they began abusing me, saying that I had stolen their diamonds.

"Speak civilly to me," I bade them. "I have here far more diamonds than any of you. *You* have to take what the eagles bring you—but I have chosen my diamonds myself, from the bottom of the valley."

I showed them my wallet, and told them how I had escaped from the valley, whereat they all marvelled. They took me to the place where they were staying together, and there I begged the merchant in whose nest I had been found (for each merchant had his own) to take as many of my big diamonds as he pleased. But he would take only one, and that the smallest of all.

"For," he said, "this one alone will make me rich enough to settle down in peace and happiness for the rest of my days."

After a while we all started off to return to our own land. We had many adventures on the way, but arrived at last at Balsora, from where I went to Bagdad. From my great wealth I gave much money to the poor, and then once again settled down to enjoy peace and comfort after my strange adventures.

THE BLACK GIANT AND THE GREAT SERPENT

I soon grew tired of my peaceful life, and longed to go voyaging again. So one day I bought some choice goods, and embarked for the third time at Balsora. When our journey was about half over, we ran into a fearful tempest which went on for several days, and drove us out of our course.

We came to an island, which the captain seemed very loath to approach, but there was no help for it. We entered the port, cast anchor, and furled our sails.

"This island and those round about are infested by a fearful multitude of dwarfs," said the captain. "They will attack us, and we must be careful not to defend ourselves nor to kill any of them, or they will swarm over us and destroy us all."

No sooner had he spoken than we saw the dwarfs swimming towards us. They were tiny savages, about two feet high, very ugly, and covered with thick red hair. There were so many of them that none of us could count them. They climbed up our ship, took down the sails, and cut away the anchor.

We watched them, and trembled, for we did not dare to defend ourselves. They hauled our ship to shore, and after making us get out, they took it away.

We made our way into the island, and found some herbs and fruit. Then, away in the distance, we saw a great palace, with a double gate of ebony. We went through this, and found ourselves in a courtyard. On one side was a heap of human bones, and on the other a great number of roasting-spits.

We were struck with horror at this sight, and fell flat to the ground, unable to move for fear.

Then, just as we were in this plight, the gate opened, and in came a great black giant, as high as a palm tree. He had one burning red eye in the middle of his forehead, and his fore-teeth stuck right out of his mouth. His under-lip hung down on his chest, and his great ears flapped over his shoulders.

We were so frightened at the sight of this monster that we lay as if we were dead.

We put to sea on our little raft

When we came to ourselves, we saw the giant sitting near by, watching us. Then he suddenly caught me up in his hand, and turned me round and round. But as I was very lean, he put me down again. He looked at all the others, and seeing that the captain was the fattest, he ate him for his supper.

This terrified us exceedingly. We heard the monster snoring all night long, but when morning came, he arose and departed. We were so frightened that we could think of no way to save ourselves. We ran about the island, taking herbs and fruit where we found them, but at night we returned to the palace, for there was no place to lie in but that.

The giant came in again, and ate another of our companions. We could do nothing but lament bitterly. The next day we determined to think of a plan of escape. I had noticed much driftwood about, and this gave me an idea.

"Let us make ourselves small rafts," I said. "Then we can perhaps throw ourselves on the mercy of the sea if no ship comes by to rescue us."

The others thought this a good idea, and we spent the day in making rafts, each big enough to take three people. At night we returned to the palace, where once more the giant ate yet another of our company.

This enraged us so much that we determined to be revenged upon the monster. So when he was asleep we heated the ends of nine roasting-spits in the fire till they were red-hot. Then we thrust them into the giant's eye and blinded him.

He awoke in great pain, and began to cry out, and to grope round for us: but we hid ourselves well, and he could not find us. At last he flung open the ebony gate and ran out howling. We followed, and made our way to the shore, resolving to wait until day, and then put out to sea on our little rafts.

Just as day dawned we saw the blind giant appear, with two others leading him. Behind came a great number of other monsters. As soon as we saw them we jumped on our rafts, and pushed off from shore. The giants saw us, and picked up great stones. These they threw at us, and their aim was so good that they sank all the rafts except the one upon which I and my two companions were.

We rowed as fast as we could, and at last we were out of reach of the giants. But then, alas! we were at the mercy of the wind and waves. We were tossed about for two days and nights, and then saw to our joy that we were being driven upon an island.

We landed in safety, and found some fruit to eat, and water to drink. Then we went to sleep on the seashore. We were awakened by a rustling noise, and to our horror saw an immense serpent. It swallowed up one of my companions, and in the greatest terror we fled away.

We came to a tall tree, and climbed it to be out of reach of the serpent, should it come that way. It was not long before the snake came hissing to the foot of the tree, and seeing us there, raised itself up against the trunk, and swallowed my comrade, who was a little lower than I was.

I was terrified, and remained in the tree for a long while. When at last I climbed down I fully expected to meet the same fate as my friends. The snake was not to be seen, however, so I hurriedly began to make myself some protection from it.

I gathered together small branches, thorns, and brambles, and bound them into faggots. These I placed all round me in a circle, and also tied some above my head in the tree. Then when night came I shut myself up in the circle. Soon the snake came along, hissing fiercely. It glided round and round the thorny rampart, but could not get in.

After a time it coiled up, and lay still, waiting for me to

We climbed the tree, out of reach of the serpent

come forth. But this I did not do, and when day dawned the serpent glided away, and left me in safety.

I was so tired, and had suffered so much from the creature's poisonous breath, that I was full of despair. I ran down to the sea, meaning to throw myself into the water, when suddenly, to my great joy, I saw a ship passing in the distance!

I shouted, and waved my turban. The crew saw me, and the captain sent out a boat to take me. Every one crowded round me when I arrived on the ship's deck, and asked me how I came to be on the island. I soon related my adventures, and the crew rejoiced that they had rescued me. The captain gave me one of his own suits, for I was all in rags.

Then the ship sailed onwards again. We touched at many ports, and at last came to Salabat. Here the merchants began to unload their goods, and the captain, seeing that I had nothing to do, came up to me.

"I have some goods here belonging to a man that has died," he said. "If you like to trade with them, I will pay you for your trouble. The money I get from the goods I shall take to the dead man's family."

I consented, for I was glad of something to do. I took the goods to the clerk of the ship, whose duty it was to enter in a book the number of bales, and the names of the merchants to whom they belonged. I presented my bales to him, and asked the captain what was the name of the merchant who had once possessed them.

"Enter them in the name of Sindbad," said the captain.

I was astonished to hear my own name, as you may imagine. I looked closely at the captain, and found, to my great amazement, that he was no other than the one in whose ship I had sailed on my second voyage, and who had left me on the island of fruit trees, when I had fallen asleep! He had much altered since I had last seen him, but there was no doubt that it was he.

"Was the merchant's name really Sindbad?" I asked.

"Yes," answered the captain. "He embarked on my ship, and sailed with me for some time. Then he, with some others, landed on an island. When we set sail again, he was left behind by mistake. His loss was not discovered till some hours later, and by that time we were driving before a strong wind, and could not return."

"You believe him to be dead, then?" I asked.

"Certainly I do," he answered.

"Now, captain," I said. "I beg you to look on me closely, and you will see that I am that Sindbad whom you left behind. I fell asleep by the brook, and when I awoke the ship was gone."

The captain looked at me in astonishment, and very soon he knew me again. He embraced me with delight, and bade me take my goods, together with the profit he had made on them.

I made much money on my homeward journey, and

when I again returned to Balsora, and went from thence to
Bagdad, I had so much wealth that I could not count it.
I gave much to the poor, and bought another great estate.
Then once again I enjoyed some years of peace and happi-
ness.

CANNIBAL ISLAND AND THE FRIENDLY KING

Not even the charms of wealth and greatness could stop
me from embarking on a fourth voyage. I had a fine journey until one day when our ship was right out at sea. A
sudden gust of wind came, and we furled our sails quickly.

It was too late. The sails were torn to rags, and the ship
driven on to a sandbank. Many of my comrades perished,
but I and a few others got hold of a plank. We were carried
to an island, and there we found fruit and spring water,
which saved us from perishing.

When we walked inland, we came to some houses.
Suddenly a number of black men rushed out, seized us, and
carried us off. We were made to sit down, and given a
certain herb to eat. My five companions, not noticing that
the black men ate none themselves, swallowed the herb
greedily. I would not even taste mine, and it was good for
me that I did not—for the effect of the herb was to make
a man lose his wits and talk nonsense.

After giving us the herb, the black men brought forth
much rice, prepared with oil of cocoa. My comrades ate
all of this, poor wretches, not having sense enough to guess
that these blacks were eaters of men; they did not see, as
I did, that they were being made fat in order to be eaten.
The herb had robbed them of their senses.

When they had become fat, the black men ate them.
But as for me, I would not touch my food, and became
thinner every day.

I presented the saddle and bridle to the king

No one took much notice of me, and I was allowed to go where I pleased; so it was not difficult for me to escape. I chose a day when all the blacks were away, except for one old man. Then I set out to run as fast as I could away from the cannibals.

I travelled for seven days, living mostly on coconuts, and on the eighth I came near the sea. Suddenly I saw a great many white people like myself, gathering pepper, which grew plentifully in that place.

I went to meet them, and they gathered round me, marvelling at my story. Then, when they had finished plucking the pepper, they set sail in their ship, taking me with them. They went to an island, and presented me to their king, who was a good and noble prince.

The island was a fine place to live in, for there was plenty of everything, and much trade was done with ships that came to the port. I was very happy there, especially as the King showed me much favour.

I noticed a very curious thing, whilst I was in that land, and that was that no one, not even the King himself, used bridle, saddle, or stirrups when riding a horse. I went to the King and asked him why.

"I do not know what you mean by saddle and bridle and stirrups," he said, puzzled. "What are these things? They are unknown in my country."

I immediately went to a workman, and told him exactly how to make a saddle, which I myself covered with gold-embroidered leather. Then I had some stirrups and a bridle made, all of which I presented to the King. I put them upon one of his horses, and when he mounted, he was so delighted with them that he made me handsome presents.

It was not long before I had made many saddles and bridles for all the nobles of the court, and soon I became rich and famous. Then one day the King called me to him and spoke to me.

"Sindbad, I love you," he said. "I wish you to do something for me."

"What is that?" I asked.

"I wish you to marry a lady of my land," he said. "Then you will settle down in my kingdom, and forget all about your own country."

I did not wish to do this, but I dared not disobey the King. Soon I was given a beautiful maiden for wife, and I lived with her in a lovely house. But I could never forget my own countrymen, and longed to return to my home.

One day a friend of mine sent me bad news. His wife had fallen ill and died. I hastened to comfort him.

"God preserve you," I said, when I saw him, "and may He grant you a long life!"

"What do you mean?" he asked in surprise. "Do you not know that I have only one hour more to live?"

"How is that?" I asked.

"It is the custom in this country to bury the live husband with the dead wife," he answered.

This filled me with horror, for, I thought, if my wife should die, I should meet my own death too.

For many days I was full of fear lest this should happen. Then, alas! what I feared came to pass. My wife fell ill, and in a short time she died.

There was no help for me. The King said that although I was a stranger to the country, I must keep to the customs, for I had married one of his ladies. Therefore, when the time came for my wife to be buried, I was taken too. The cavalcade went up the mountains, and in my despair I suddenly broke away and ran for my life.

A sea-animal blundered against me in the dark

I came to a pit whose top was covered by a stone. I lifted it up, and let myself down. No one discovered me, and I stayed there for several days. Then something came blundering against me in the dark. It was some sea-animal that had come up from the seashore, which I had not known was near.

I followed the creature along a narrow, winding passage, which pierced through the heart of the mountain right down to the sea. How thankful I was to see daylight again, and to breathe the fresh sea air!

For two or three days I stayed on the seashore. Then I saw a vessel that had left the port of the island, and I hailed her. She saw me, and sent a boat to bring me to her. I told the captain I had been shipwrecked, for I did not want him to send me back to the King. Happily, he believed my story, and allowed me to sail with him on his ship.

We went to many ports, and by good fortune I did some profitable trade with goods that the captain kindly gave me. When at last I arrived at Balsora again, I had infinite riches, and was able to make great gifts to the poor and to the church. Then I settled down happily to enjoy my kindred and friends, eager to forget how near I had been to death.

THE OLD MAN OF THE SEA

After some time I decided to build myself a ship, and go voyaging once more. When my vessel was ready, I embarked on board, taking with me many other merchants and their goods.

We sailed with a fair wind, and were some weeks on the open sea. The first place we came to was a desert island, and there we found an enormous egg. It was a roc egg, and the young bird inside was on the point of hatching.

"Do not meddle with the egg," I warned the merchants who were with me. "The parent rocs are dangerous."

But they took no heed of my words. They broke open the egg with their hatchets, dragged out the young bird piece by piece, and roasted it.

They had hardly finished their feasting when two large black clouds appeared in the sky.

"Here are the parent rocs!" shouted the captain. "Let us embark again with all speed before they try to revenge themselves on us!"

We hurriedly re-embarked and set sail. We watched the two rocs find their broken egg, and heard them bewail it with a terrible noise. Then suddenly they arose in the air, and flew off in the direction from which they had come. We sailed away as fast as we could, but alas! It was of no use.

Soon the giant birds returned, each one holding in its beak a tremendous stone. They flew immediately above our vessel, and one dropped its stone. If the steersman had not cleverly turned our ship about, we should have been struck. Then the other roc dropped the stone it held. It fell right on to our vessel, split it into a thousand pieces, and sank it. All the merchants on board were either killed or sunk.

I sank down through the water, but was able to take hold of a piece of wood. I swam with this to an island, and got ashore. I found there were trees everywhere, full of delicious fruit—indeed the island was like a beautiful garden.

As I wandered inland, I saw an old man sitting upon the bank of a stream. I thought he must have been shipwrecked like myself, and I went forward to greet him. He did not speak in reply, but signed to me to take him upon my back, pointing over the stream as if he wished to cross the water, and gather fruit on the other side.

The old man forced me to carry him about

He seemed very weak and feeble, so I placed him on my back, and carried him across the stream. Then I bade him get down, and stooped so that he might do so. But instead he slipped his legs round my neck, and gripped me so tightly with them that I was nearly strangled. I saw that his skin was like that of a cow, and then, so tightly did he clasp his legs round my throat that I fell to the ground in a faint.

When I came to my senses, the old man was still about my neck. He kicked me roughly, and made me get up. I did so, and he forced me to walk about under the fruit trees, so that he might pick what he wanted.

I had no rest from him that day, but was forced to carry him about with me all the time. When night came, and I lay down, he lay down with me, but would not leave go his hold on my throat.

Every day I spent in the same way, carrying the horrible old creature about with me. I led a miserable life, and could not think how to get rid of him.

Then one day I found some empty gourds. I took up the largest and cleaned it. Then I pressed into it some grapes, and I left the juice there for some days. When I next came to the gourd, I drank the grape-wine I had made, and found it so good that I sang and shouted for joy.

The old man signed to me to give him some. I made him a gourd-full, and he drank it all off at once. He was not used to the drink, and it stupefied him and made him sleepy. When I found that he did not grip me so tightly with his legs, I gave a sudden jolt, and jerked him to the ground. He lay there without moving, and taking up a stone I slew the wicked creature without pity.

I ran down to the seashore, rejoicing with all my heart that I was free of my horrible burden. On the beach I met the crew of a ship who had landed to take in water. They were amazed to see me, and to hear my adventure.

"You fell into the hands of the Old Man of the Sea," they said. "No man has ever escaped from him before. He has strangled many hundreds of poor shipwrecked sailors, and richly deserved his death."

I put to sea with the crew, and soon we came to a great city. Here one of the merchants of the ship, with whom I had become friends, gave me a great bag.

"Go with the folk of this city," he said, "and they will take you to gather coconuts. Thus you will be able to obtain goods which you can trade in other places."

I took the bag, and went with the townsfolk, who were likewise laden with bags. We set out on a journey, and after a time came to a forest of great, tall trees, whose trunks were so smooth that it was impossible to climb them to reach the fruit.

I wondered how we were to get the coconuts, but it was not long before I saw the way. The trees were full of monkeys, who seemed very angry at our arrival. The merchants took up stones, and flung them at the furious animals. This enraged them to such an extent that they plucked the coconuts and threw them down at us. Thus all we had to do was to gather up the nuts and place them in our bags. We soon had a great number, as you can imagine.

I spent many days in this way, till I had a vast amount of nuts. Then, when a ship called into the port, I embarked on board, taking my nuts with me. We sailed to the Isle of Comari, where I exchanged my goods for pepper and wood of aloes. I then hired divers to go pearl-fishing for me, and they brought me up some very large, pure pearls.

With these goods I sailed to Balsora, and when I again reached Bagdad I sold my pepper, wood of aloes, and pearls for vast sums. I then gave away the tenth of my wealth to the poor, and once more settled down to enjoy my riches.

THE HILL OF THE ELEPHANTS

For some time I enjoyed a quiet life. Then one day the Caliph sent for me, and I hastened to his court.

"Sindbad," he said, "I wish you to take ship and return to the King of the Isle of Serendid, taking with you a letter from me and some rich presents."

I was full of dismay when I heard this, for I had no wish for any more voyages or adventures. But the Caliph commanded that I should go, so I dared not disobey.

Once again I went to Balsora, and embarked on a ship. I had a very happy voyage, and arrived quite safely at Serendid. The king was delighted to see me again, and was much pleased to receive the Caliph's letter and gifts.

The time soon came for me to depart once more. I bade farewell to the king, who gave me a rich present for myself, and then embarked to return speedily to Balsora.

But on the way much misfortune came upon us. Pirates attacked our ship, and took it. Those that defended themselves were killed, but I and some others who remained quiet were spared. We were all stripped of our clothes and given horrible rags to wear. Then the pirates took us to a far-off land and sold us as slaves.

A rich merchant bought me, and treated me well. He asked me if I knew any trade that I could follow.

"I am a merchant," I replied. "The pirates robbed me, and took me prisoner."

"Can you shoot with bow and arrows?" he asked.

"I used to, when I was young," I answered. "I do not think I have forgotten how to do so, even now."

My master thereupon gave me a bow and arrows, put me behind him on an elephant, and took me to a great forest. At last he stopped, and showed me a large tree.

"Climb up this tree," he said. "Elephants will come by, and you must shoot at them. If you kill one, come and tell me."

He left me there, and returned the way he had come. The next morning a great number of elephants came by. I shot my arrows among them, and slew one. When the great beasts had all gone, I ran to tell my master, who was full of joy to think that I had already killed an elephant for him.

We returned to the forest, and dug a hole in which we buried the great creature, for my master meant to come and get the ivory tusks later. Then he bade me climb my tree again, and continue my shooting.

For two months I did this, and shot many elephants. Then one day a dreadful thing happened. All the elephants in the forest came to my tree, and stood around me!

The earth shook under their feet, and the noise was terrible. They surrounded my tree, and stood staring at me, with their great trunks stretched out. I was so frightened that my bow and arrows fell from my hands.

Then the biggest of the elephants advanced to my tree, and wrapped his trunk around it. He pulled it straight up by the roots, and flung it to the ground. I fell with it, and lay like a dead man. The elephant picked me up, and put me on his back, then started off through the forest, followed by all the rest.

I was too terrified to move, and thought surely I was going to my death. After some time I felt myself being put down on the ground. Then all the elephants went away and left me by myself.

I sat up and looked around me. Imagine my astonishment when I saw that I was on a long, high hill, covered with the bones and tusks of hundreds of elephants!

"This must be the hill where they come to die!" I cried. "Oh, the wise beasts! They have brought me here to show me that I can get tusks from dead animals, and so do not need to slay the living!"

I at once went to seek my master, and after travelling for twenty-four hours, I came to him. He was delighted to see me, having thought that I had been killed by the elephants, like most of his other slaves.

When I took him to the hill of the elephants, he was filled with astonishment and delight.

"Now my fortune is made!" he cried. "And yours too, O Sindbad, for I will see to that myself!"

We spent some months in filling his warehouses with ivory, and then, when a ship called at the port, I went aboard, meaning to return home. My master gave me a great cargo of ivory and many rich presents. Then I set sail, rejoicing that my adventure had ended so well.

As soon as my ship touched at the mainland I went ashore, for I thought I would prefer to go overland to Balsora, rather than over sea, for I did now know what other strange adventure might come to me on the water. I sold my ivory, and with the great sums I got by it, I bought wonderful presents for my friends.

Then I set out in company with a large caravan of merchants, and at last came safely to Bagdad. I went at once to the Caliph, who was glad to see me, for he had thought I must be dead, since I was such a long time away.

And now, for the last time, I settled down in peace and happiness, resolved never again to set out on a voyage. Thus ends the last adventure of old Sindbad the Sailor.

Aladdin and the Wonderful Lamp

THERE once lived in China a lazy boy called Aladdin. He was the despair of his poor mother, for he would not work, but ran about the streets all day long. His father was dead, so his mother was forced to work for them both.

One day a magician came to the city. He saw Aladdin, and looked at him closely.

"This lad will do well for my purpose," he said. "I will pretend to be his uncle, then he will obey me, and do what I wish."

So he went up to Aladdin and embraced him, saying, with tears in his eyes, that he was his uncle, and had come to find the wife and son of his dear brother, whom he had heard was now dead.

Aladdin was delighted to think he had an uncle who was richly dressed, and who might be wealthy and generous. He took him home to his mother, and the magician paid for a splendid meal.

"I will set Aladdin up in a fine shop," he promised. "I will come to-morrow and take him to a tailor's, where I will buy him a magnificent new suit."

Aladdin and his mother were so overjoyed that they could hardly sleep that night. In the morning the magician came as he had promised, and bought Aladdin a richly embroidered dress.

"Now we will go walking," he said. "I want to give you some advice, nephew, and therefore we will spend the day together."

He took Aladdin through the city, talking to him wisely

Aladdin

all the time, as an uncle might talk to his favourite
nephew. At last they passed right out of the city and
came to the country. Still the magician led Aladdin on, and
only stopped when they arrived in a valley between two
mountains.

"Now I am going to show you something strange that
no one has seen before," said the magician. "Gather me
some sticks, Aladdin, and we will light a fire."

Aladdin obeyed. Soon a great fire was blazing. The
magician threw some powder upon the flames, turned himself about, and pronounced some magic words.

Suddenly the earth shook, and opened just in front of
Aladdin. In the space that appeared was a stone with a
brass ring in the middle. The lad was so frightened that he
turned to run away, but the magician caught hold of him,
and boxed his ears angrily.

"I have brought you here to fulfil my commands," he said. "Do as you are told, and I will make you rich."

Aladdin listened in surprise. When he heard that he might be made rich, he begged his supposed uncle to tell him what he must do.

"Pull up this stone," said the magician. "Go down the steps to the door at the end. Open it, and you will find yourself in a beautiful palace. Go through three vast halls, into the fourth. In a corner you will see a lamp hanging. Take it down, and bring it to me."

Aladdin promised to do as he was bid. The magician pulled a ring off his finger, and slipped it on Aladdin's.

"Wear this," he said. "It will keep you from harm."

The youth pulled up the stone, and saw a flight of steps going downwards. He ran down them, and came to a door, which he opened. He passed through it into a beautiful palace. Through three vast halls he went, and came to the fourth, where in a corner hung the lamp of which the magician had told him.

He took it, and fastened it to his belt. Then he saw a wonderful garden outside the hall, with trees bearing strange fruit, for they were hung with rubies, emeralds, diamonds, and sapphires. Aladdin ran to them, and filled his pockets full of the precious stones.

Then he went back to the opening where he had left the magician. The old man was awaiting him impatiently, and as soon as he saw Aladdin, he sharply commanded him to pass him the lamp.

"It is fastened to my belt," replied the lad. "Wait till I get out of here, uncle."

Then the magician flew into a rage, and ordered Aladdin to do as he was bid. But the youth would not give him the lamp until he was outside.

The magician stamped his foot in fury. He turned to the

fire, which was still burning, and flung a pinch of powder on it, pronouncing two fearful words of magic at the same time. Immediately the stone closed up the entrance to the underground cave, and poor Aladdin was a prisoner!

He called and pleaded, but it was of no use. The magician had gone. Aladdin ran down the steps to enter the palace again, but found that the door to it was shut. He was indeed a prisoner. In despair he clasped his hands together, and in doing so rubbed the ring which the magician had given him.

Then a most surprising thing happened! An enormous genie rose out of the earth, and bowed down before Aladdin!

"What do you wish?" he asked. "I am the slave of the ring, and must obey you in everything."

"Then take me from this place," said Aladdin, after he had overcome his astonishment. At once the genie caught hold of him, and in a trice Aladdin found himself outside the cave, seated on the place where the stone had once been.

He made his way back to the city, and soon arrived home, where he told his mother all that had happened. Then, being very tired, he went to bed.

Next morning he awoke feeling hungry, and begged his mother to get him breakfast. She replied that there was none in the house, but she would go and sell some cotton she had made.

"Wait a moment, Mother," said Aladdin. "I have here an old lamp that I got for that wicked magician. Take it and sell it. That should bring us enough for breakfast."

"It is very dirty," said his mother. "I will polish it."

She took a rag and rubbed it hard. Immediately a gigantic genie appeared, and spoke to her in a voice of thunder.

"What do you wish? I am the slave of the lamp, and must obey you in everything."

Aladdin's mother was so frightened that she fell in a faint

An enormous genie rose out of the earth

on the floor. Aladdin snatched the lamp from her, and gave his commands to the genie.

"I am hungry," he said. "Bring me breakfast."

The genie disappeared, but soon returned again with a large silver basin on his head, and twelve covered silver dishes containing all kinds of delicious food. These he placed before Aladdin, then bowed and disappeared.

The youth soon brought his mother to her senses, and they sat down together to enjoy the meal, marvelling at the strange happenings of the last two days.

Such was the beginning of Aladdin's good fortune. He and his mother now had no lack of good things, and lived in great comfort.

Then one day Aladdin saw the Sultan's daughter, the beautiful Badroulbadour. She was so charming, so lovely, so enchanting that the youth fell head over heels in love with her. Nothing could content him but that he must make her his wife.

His mother laughed when she heard this, but Aladdin would not alter his purpose. He bade her go to the Sultan, taking with her the jewels he had picked from the strange trees in the underground cave. She was to give the Sultan these, and ask that the princess might become the wife of her son.

The poor woman, who felt certain that the Sultan would be angry with her for asking such a thing, at last agreed to go. She put the jewels in a china dish, covered them with a damask cloth, and set off.

The Sultan received her, and she uncovered the dish, begging him to accept the present that her son had sent him.

"He beseeches you to give him your daughter in marriage," she said.

The Sultan hardly heard her. He was gazing at the marvellous jewels in the china dish. Never before had he seen such treasures. Each one of them was worth more than all the gold in his coffers.

"My son requests the honour of your daughter's hand in marriage," repeated Aladdin's mother, seeing the Sultan's amazement.

"Tell him he shall have her if he can send me forty golden dishes full of jewels like these, carried by forty black slaves, who shall be led by as many young and handsome white ones!" said the Sultan.

The woman left the palace in delight, for she knew that the genie could obtain these things. She told Aladdin what the Sultan had said, and he was overjoyed.

He rubbed the lamp, and when the genie appeared, he commanded him to fulfil the Sultan's wish, and also to dress himself and his mother in rich and magnificent clothing. This was all done in the twinkling of an eye.

Soon the astonished people of the city saw a great procession of black and white slaves walking to the Sultan's palace, and at the head were Aladdin and his mother dressed in superb robes. The Sultan received them with delight, for he thought surely Aladdin must be a very great prince.

"You shall marry my daughter to-morrow," he promised. "Meanwhile, let me entertain you to-day in my palace."

Aladdin spent the day with the Sultan. When he returned home he rubbed the wonderful lamp again, and commanded the genie to build him a marvellous palace opposite the Sultan's. It was to be of silver and gold, and the windows were to be studded with precious stones. There were to be servants of all kinds, and also a treasury filled with bags of gold and silver.

In the morning the Sultan was amazed to see a magnificent palace glittering in the distance. He felt more certain than ever that Aladdin must be a rich and mighty prince, and he was overjoyed to think that his daughter would have such a powerful husband.

The beautiful Princess Badroulbadour was married to Aladdin that day, and proudly he took her home with him to his palace. Very happy were they both, the princess because her husband was so rich and handsome, and Aladdin because he had for wife the sweetest and loveliest maiden in the land.

They lived happily together for some time. Then one day Aladdin went out hunting, and the princess was left alone. It so happened that the magician came into the city that morning, anxious to find out what had happened to Aladdin. He felt certain that the youth had perished in the underground cave, but he wished to make sure.

Very soon, by means of his magic art, he discovered that

The maid brought the lamp to the princess

Aladdin had escaped, taking the wonderful lamp with him. When he came to the palace that the genie had built, he at once knew that it was a magic one, and guessed that Aladdin was the owner. He was amazed when he heard that the poor peasant boy he had left in the cave had become the Sultan's son-in-law, and had won the beautiful princess for wife.

He was angry, and determined to punish Aladdin. He bought a dozen new brass lamps, and put them into a basket. Then he went slowly down the street by the palace, crying out, "New lamps for old! New lamps for old!"

At once children ran round him laughing, for they had never heard of any one giving new things for old before. Soon there was a mob round the old man, and the princess, leaning from her window, saw the crowd, and wondered what the excitement was.

Her servants told her.

"It is a pedlar who is giving new lamps for old!" they said. "Mistress, there is an old lamp in your lord's room. Shall we not exchange it for a new one? Whoever owns the old will be pleased to find a new one in its place."

"Fetch it, and change it then," said the princess, anxious to see if the pedlar really meant what he said.

No sooner did the magician see the servant bringing out the old lamp to him than he knew it was the one he wanted. He seized it, threw a new one at the girl, and hurried away.

When he came to a quiet corner he rubbed it. At once the genie appeared, and was commanded to transport Aladdin's palace into the middle of the desert. This he did, much to the fear and astonishment of the princess and her ladies.

The Sultan was amazed to see the palace gone. When Aladdin returned from the hunt, he too was filled with astonishment. He soon guessed what had happened, and resolved to defeat the magician as soon as possible.

He rubbed the ring on his finger, and when the slave appeared he commanded him to bring the palace back again.

"Lord, I am not so mighty as the slave of the lamp," answered the genie. "I cannot do that."

"Then take me to the place where the palace stands," said Aladdin impatiently.

This was soon done. Aladdin found himself on the steps of his own palace, and swiftly he ran up them, and made his way to the princess, who was overjoyed to see him.

"Hide behind this curtain," she said. "When the magician comes to see me, you can surprise him, and slay him."

Aladdin did as she bade him. When he heard the magician enter, he sprang out, and without mercy slew the wicked man instantly. Then he took the wonderful lamp from him, and rubbed it.

At once the genie appeared, and bowed low.

"Take this palace back to its rightful place," commanded Aladdin. Immediately it arose in the air, and in a trice returned to its place in the city of the Sultan.

How overjoyed he was to see Aladdin and the princess once again! Bells rang out through the city, and a great festival was proclaimed. All the people made holiday and rejoiced.

When the Sultan died Aladdin became ruler, and he and his lovely princess lived happily together to the end of their days.

The Enchanted Horse

LONG AGO, when the Emperor of Persia was holding a festival, an Indian came to the foot of his throne, and bowed himself to the ground. With him he brought a magnificent horse, which, although it looked as if it were real, was artificial.

"Lord," said the Indian, "I bring you the most wonderful thing in the world—a horse that will transport its rider through the air to any place that he wishes to go."

"Let me see this wonder," commanded the Emperor. "Do you see that hill yonder? Bid your horse take you there, and, so that I shall know you have truly been there, bring me back a palm-leaf from the tree that grows at the bottom of the hill."

The Indian leapt on to the horse's back, and turned a peg in its neck. At once the wonderful thing rose up into the air, and flew like the wind to the distant hill. In a short time the Indian returned, bearing in his hand a palm-leaf.

The Emperor was amazed.

"What do you want for this wonder of yours?" he asked.

"But one thing," said the Indian. "Grant me your daughter as wife, and you shall have the horse."

The Emperor's son, who was near by, was angry to hear the request of the Indian.

"What!" he cried. "Does this insolent juggler think that the princess would be given to him as wife?"

"Peace, my son," commanded the Emperor. "I certainly shall not grant him his ridiculous request, but maybe I can give him something else which will please him as much. Before I make my proposal to him, mount the horse yourself, and see what you think of its powers."

The prince ran to the horse, and before the Indian could help him up, or give him any advice, he leapt into the saddle, and turned the peg in the horse's neck. At once it rose into the air, and flew away to the west.

The Indian cried out in fear, for he knew that the prince had no idea how to manage the horse. He flung himself down before the Emperor, and begged him not to punish him if the prince did not return.

The Emperor turned pale. He waited for the horse to bring back the prince, but it had vanished completely, and there was no sign of its return.

"Throw this Indian into prison," he commanded. "There he shall remain, and if my son does not come back, his head shall be cut off!"

The wretched Indian was flung into prison and there he lay, bewailing his fate and fearing death at any moment.

The prince at first enjoyed his ride very much. When he thought he had been away long enough, he turned the peg in the horses' neck again. To his surprise and fear, the horse did not return, but went on flying higher than ever in the sky. Soon the prince lost sight of the earth, and could not tell where he was.

At last night came, and stars twinkled down. The prince suddenly found another little peg, just behind the animal's right ear. He turned it, and was delighted to find that the horse at once began to descend.

Soon it came to rest on something hard. The prince leapt off its back, and found that he was on the flat roof of a magnificent palace wherein dwelt the Princess of Bengal. He found a flight of steps leading downwards, and descended them.

He came to a big room where many black slaves lay sleeping on the floor. He tiptoed between them, and came to another room. On a raised bed lay a fair princess, more beautiful than any maiden the prince had ever seen.

The prince leapt into the saddle and flew away

He made his way softly to her bedside, and gazed on her. Then he gently touched her snow-white arm. She awoke and looked in surprise at the handsome prince by her side.

"Madam," said the prince, "do not be afraid. By the strangest adventure imaginable, I, the son of the Emperor of Persia, have arrived here at your palace. I pray you to give me your protection."

The princess listened in astonishment. Then she awoke her slaves, and bade them give the prince food and drink, and then conduct him to a bed.

"You shall tell me your story in the morning," she said.

When day dawned the princess arose and made herself even more beautiful than she was already. Then she sent for the prince to come to her, and listened in surprise to the strange tale he told her.

"You must spend some time in my kingdom before you return," she said. This the prince was only too glad to do, for he had straightway fallen in love with the fair princess.

For two months he remained with her, and then he said that he must return to his father.

"Come with me, I beg of you," he entreated. "I love you, and would marry you. Let me take you to my father, the Emperor of Persia."

The maiden, who had fallen madly in love with the handsome prince, soon consented. Next morning, very early,

On a raised bed lay a fair princess

they arose and went to the enchanted horse. The prince mounted on its back, and placed the princess safely before him. Then, turning the peg in its neck, they set out on their journey through the air.

When they arrived at the kingdom of the Persian Emperor, the prince made the horse descend.

"This palace at which we are now arrived is the summer palace of my father," he said. "Remain here, I pray you, until I have prepared the Emperor for your coming. I will then send to fetch you."

The prince gave the enchanted horse to a groom, and then mounted one of his own horses. He rode off, and soon came to his father's city. The people gave him a great welcome, cheering him, and running beside his horse in delight.

The Emperor was overjoyed to see his son again, and embraced him tenderly. When he heard of his strange adventure, he was amazed.

"We will go to fetch your princess with great pomp and splendour," he said. "Let us make ready now. In the meantime, the Indian to whom the horse belonged shall be freed."

Now, as soon as the Indian was freed, he asked what had happened. His jailer told him, and an evil plan came into the Indian's mind. He would revenge himself on the Emperor and the prince!

Without delay, he ran to the summer palace, where the princess awaited the prince.

"Tell the princess that I have been sent to carry her on the enchanted horse to the prince, her lover," he said to the man guarding the animal.

The princess believed the message to be true, and at once came out and mounted the horse with the Indian. He turned the peg in its neck, and they rose into the air. As they flew off, they were seen by the Emperor and the prince, who were on their way to fetch the princess.

In amazement and despair the poor prince stood and watched the Indian flying off with his lady. Then he began to weep bitterly, for he did not know where she was being taken to, nor how he should find her again.

He dressed himself as a peasant, and went wandering through many lands, seeking for his princess, but not for a long while did he obtain news of her.

Meanwhile the Indian had flown far away with the frightened maiden, who knew, as soon as she saw the prince down below, that the Indian had played her false.

After some hours, the wicked man brought the horse down into a wood, near the capital city of Cashmire.

"I will get you some food, fair lady," he said, "and then I will find some one to marry us."

"I will never marry you!" cried the princess in horror. She tried to run away but the Indian ran after her and caught her. She began to shriek for help, and happily her cries were at once heard.

The Sultan of Cashmire and his men were passing through the wood, returning from a hunt. They ran to the fair lady's rescue, and one of the men slew the wicked Indian. The princess was full of gratitude, and thanked the Sultan with all her heart.

"Come with me to my palace," said the Sultan. "You shall stay there and be well looked after. Tell me your story as we ride through the wood."

The princess told her story, and the Sultan looked with great interest at the enchanted horse, which he commanded to be taken along with them. As soon as they reached his palace he took the princess to some beautiful rooms, gave her a great number of slaves, and left her.

The princess felt sure that the Sultan would send her back to her prince without delay, and went to bed very happily. She was awakened next morning by the sound of drums and trumpets, and asked her slaves what the joyful sounds were for.

"It is your wedding day!" they said. "The Sultan, our master, means to marry you to-day!"

The poor princess fell back in a faint at this news. She had no idea that the Sultan had fallen in love with her, and had resolved to marry her immediately. When she came to her senses she determined to pretend she was mad, and then perhaps the Sultan would put off the wedding.

So she said strange things, and flew at every one who came near her. Her slaves were dismayed, and sent word to the Sultan. The princess sang and gabbled and made as if she would fly at him too, so that he departed in horror, and gave orders that the marriage was not to be held until the princess was better.

But she became worse rather than better, and the Sultan sent for the wisest doctors in the land. They could do

The prince and the princess set out on their journey

nothing with her, and gave her up in despair, for they did not guess that her madness was all a pretence.

One day the prince, who was still seeking for his lady, heard news of a princess of Bengal who was mad, and wondered if it could be his long-lost love. He made his way to Cashmire, and at last came to the Sultan's city. He sent word to him that he thought he could cure the princess if he could have a little time alone with her.

The Sultan, eager to try any one's skill, consented to this. The prince, disguised as a doctor, entered the room where the princess sat. She made as if she would fly at him, but he spoke softly to her.

"I am your own prince," he said. "I come to rescue you. Do not show that you know me, in case any one is spying upon us."

The princess was overjoyed. She sat quietly, and the prince, in a low voice, told her all his tale. Then he went to speak with the Sultan.

"Lord," he said. "How comes it that the Princess of Bengal should be here, so far from her own country?"

"She came on an enchanted horse," answered the Sultan. "I have it here still."

"Ah!" said the prince, who had made a cunning plan. "Now I see what is the cause of the princess's illness. Some of the horse's enchantment has entered into her and made her mad. I can cure her, if you will permit me to mount her upon the horse, whilst I use my magic near by."

The Sultan promised to do all that the prince wished, for he was full of happiness to think that the princess might soon be well enough to marry him.

"Bring out the enchanted horse and stand it in the great square of the city," said the prince. "Then bid the princess dress herself richly, and adorn herself with the most beautiful jewels that you possess. Proclaim to your people that the princess is to be cured, and let them come to see the sight, for it will be a marvellous one."

All was done as the prince commanded. The horse was brought out into the great square, and every one assembled to see the princess cured. Soon she herself appeared, covered with jewels. The prince took her hand, and led her to the horse. She mounted it, and sat there, waiting.

Then the prince caused a great many vessels full of fire to be placed round the horse. He threw on the flames a powder which sent out a strong smell and a dark smoke. Then he ran round the horse three times, pretending to mutter magic words.

The Sultan sent for the wisest doctors in the land

By this time the vessels had sent out such dense clouds of smoke that neither the horse nor the princess could be seen. The prince jumped up behind his lady, turned the peg in the horse's neck, and at once rose into the air!

The Sultan saw them when they were high up, and was filled with the most terrible rage and grief. But he could do nothing.

It was not long before the prince and princess arrived in Persia, and were greatly welcomed by the Emperor and all his people. They were married the same day, and every one rejoiced at their happiness. They dwelt together in great content, and were happy to the end of their days.

Ali Baba and the Forty Thieves

THERE once lived two brothers called Cassim and Ali Baba. One was rich and the other was poor. Ali was the poor brother, and got his living by cutting wood in the forest nearby, and carrying it into the town upon his three asses.

One day, when he had loaded his asses, he saw a crowd of well-armed, well-mounted horsemen coming in the distance. He at once guessed them to be robbers, and in a panic he hid his asses, and climbed up a tree that grew above a large rock in the hillside.

There he hid, hoping that the robbers would pass by without seeing him. To his surprise they rode right up to the rock over which his tree grew, and dismounted. The leader went up to the rock and said, in a loud and commanding voice—

"Open Sesame!"

At once the rock slid aside, showing an opening. The robbers disappeared inside, and did not come out for some time. When they did, they galloped away.

Ali Baba slid down from the tree, and ran to the rock. "Open Sesame!" he cried. The rock slid aside again, and lo and behold! Instead of a gloomy cavern, Ali Baba saw a spacious room in which were piled gold, silver, jewels, brocades and silks.

Ali hurriedly took as many bags of gold as his three asses would carry, and went to the entrance of the cave. He found that it was shut, but when he pronounced the words "Open Sesame!" again, the rock once more opened, and he ran out. It closed behind him, and Ali Baba looked for his three asses. He loaded them with the bags of gold, and then set off for the town.

When he undid the bags and showed his wife all the gold he had brought, she was so astonished that she could not speak a word.

"Let us bury it in the garden to-night," she said at last. "But first I must know how much we have. There is too much to count, so I will borrow a measure from your brother Cassim's wife, and measure it."

She ran to borrow what she wanted. Cassim's wife, knowing how poor Ali Baba was, wondered what he needed a measure for. So, being a curious woman, she put a little suet at the bottom of her measure, hoping that a little of whatever Ali was measuring would stick to the bottom, and so tell her what she wanted to know.

Ali's wife measured the gold, and then went to return the measure. Judge of the astonishment of Cassim's wife when she found a gold piece sticking to the bottom of her measure! She at once ran to Cassim and showed him.

"Your brother must be far richer than you are if he has to measure his gold, instead of counting it," she said. "Go and find out where he gets it from."

So Cassim went to Ali Baba, and told him what his wife had found.

"I am your brother," he said. "You must share your good fortune with me."

Then Ali Baba, who was always good-tempered, and willing to do any one a good turn, told his brother everything, even to the words that opened the treasure cave.

Cassim at once resolved to go to the cave before Ali Baba went again, and take from it all the treasure there was. So next morning, very early, he saddled his ass, and rode off, followed by ten mules, each carrying a large empty chest. He easily found the rock, and on saying the words

Ali Baba watched the robbers enter the cave

"Open Sesame!" saw it open, and display the treasure
cave.

He went in, overjoyed to see so much wealth. The door
shut behind him, but as he knew the words to open it
again he thought nothing of that. He began to get together
all the gold and jewels he could see. When he had got
enough to fill the ten chests, he went to the rock that
closed the entrance of the cave.

Then alas for Cassim! He could not remember the words
that opened the cave! Sesame was the name of a certain
grain, and Cassim, remembering that he must say the name
of a grain, said "Open Barley!"

The rock remained shut. Then Cassim tried again.
"Open Oats!" he shouted. But the rock did not move.

Cassim fell into a panic, and shouted the names of all the grains he could think of, but never once did he hit on the right one.

After some time, the robbers returned, and saw the ten mules outside the cave. They at once knew that some one was inside. The Captain, as soon as the rock opened at his command, rushed in and slew poor Cassim.

"Maybe he is the only one who knows our secret," he said. "But in case any one else shares it with him, we will show how dreadful our revenge is. We will cut this man's body into four pieces, and put two on each side of the door to warn any intruder of our severity."

This was done, and the robbers once more rode off.

Now Cassim's wife began to get very uneasy when her husband did not come back. She sent for Ali Baba and begged him to go to the cave, and see if he was there. Ali went at once, and when he found the body of his brother, he was full of sorrow.

"We must let no one know of this," he said to Cassim's weeping wife. "You must say that he has died of an illness. To-morrow we will give him a funeral, but first I must find some one who will sew these four pieces together, so that my poor brother may rest in peace."

Ali Baba did not dare to go out and find some one himself, so he let Morgiana, a slave of Cassim's, into the dreadful secret. The girl promised to do all she could, and ran out to find a cobbler. Soon she came to one called Baba Mustapha, who sat in the market mending shoes.

"Come with me," she said, "I have a piece of work for you. See, here is a gold coin. You shall have another when the work is finished. But I must bind your eyes, Baba Mustapha, for you must not know to what place you are going."

The old cobbler consented. Morgiana bound his eyes, and led him to her dead master's house. There she bade him sew the four pieces together, which he did neatly and quickly. Then she bound his eyes, and led him back to his stall again.

Cassim was given a fine funeral, and no one guessed that he had been killed by robbers, but all thought he had died of an illness. Ali Baba moved to Cassim's house, and he and his wife enjoyed their new riches.

Now when the robbers discovered that Cassim's body had been taken away, they were in a fright, for they knew that some one had learnt of their hiding-place, and was taking away their gold.

"One of you must dress as a traveller, and go into the town to see if you can hear of any one who has been cut to pieces," said the Captain. "Then we shall soon find his friend or his brother, or whoever it is that has taken away the body."

So one of the robbers disguised himself, and set off in the early morning. It happened that he stood by Baba Mustapha's stall, when he entered the market, and he watched the old man's nimble fingers with admiration.

"Old man," he said, "you must have good eyes to see so well at your stitching, for indeed it is hardly light yet."

The cobbler laughed. "My eyes are as good as my fingers!" he boasted. "Why, my friend, I sewed together a body the other day, and had not as much light to do so as there is now!"

The robber looked at him sharply, for he knew that by chance he had hit on the right person to help him.

"Tell me more about this," he said.

But Baba Mustapha would say nothing further.

"Lead me to this place, and I will give you gold," said the robber.

"I was blindfold, so I do not know where it was," said Mustapha.

"Here is gold," said the robber. "Let me blindfold you, and maybe you can remember the way."

He at last won the cobbler's consent, and the old man

led the way blindfold to Cassim's house, where Ali Baba now lived. The robber marked the door with a white cross, and rewarded his guide with more gold. Then he ran to tell the Captain of his discovery.

Now Morgiana, the slave, happening to come out of the house on an errand, noticed the white cross on the door. "This bodes no good for my master," she thought.

Ali Baba loaded his ass with Treasure

So, taking a piece of white chalk, she made crosses on many other doors up and down the street.

When the robber Captain came to find the door he was astonished to find a great many with white crosses on, and could not, of course, discover in which house lived the man who knew his secret. In rage he returned to his men and slew the wretched robber who had marked the door with a cross. Then he sent a second man to the cobbler.

Baba Mustapha, blindfold, led him to the door of Ali's house. He marked it with a tiny red cross in the corner, and returned rejoicing to his master. But Morgiana, who was now on the look-out, saw the cross with her sharp eyes, and straightway marked all the other doors near by in the same way.

The robber Captain was full of rage when he saw this, and he slew the second robber. Then he determined to go to the town himself and find out. So once again the old cobbler led a robber to Ali Baba's door. This time there was no cross made, for the Captain simply examined it very carefully, till he felt certain he would know it again; then he returned to his men.

"Go and buy nineteen mules and thirty-eight oil-jars," he commanded. "Fill one with oil, and then come to me."

This was done. The Captain made his thirty-seven men get into the oil-jars, and then he tied up the tops of them. He loaded the nineteen mules with two jars each and set off to go to Ali Baba's, meaning to ask for a night's shelter there, and then slay all who were in the house.

Ali Baba willingly gave the supposed oil merchant shelter, and told him to put his jars in the yard. The Captain commanded his men to leap out as soon as he called them, and then left them.

Now Morgiana the slave was preparing a fine dinner for her master and his guest. As she was in the middle of it, her lamp went out, for there was no more oil left. She remembered that there were oil jars in the yard, and picking up her lamp, she ran out to fill it from a jar.

As she ran to one, a voice spoke from within it. "Is it time?" said the voice.

Then Morgiana guessed that the oil merchant was not what he seemed, and as soon as she had heard voices from thirty-seven of the jars, each asking the same question, she knew that her master's guest was the Captain of the thieves who had brought his robbers with him. To every man she answered, "Not yet, but presently," then she filled her lamp from the one real jar of oil and ran to the kitchen.

She took her big kettle and filled it with oil, which she boiled over the fire. Then, running to every jar containing a robber, she poured in enough oil to stifle and kill him. This done, she went on with her preparation of the dinner.

The Captain thought that the time had now come to call his men. He went to the room that had been given to him, and leaned from the window.

"It is time," he called, in a low voice. There was no answer. He called again—and then, surprised and dismayed,

The robbers in the jars

ran into the yard. He peeped into the jars and found all his men dead. Then, full of fear, he went back to the house again, determined to kill Ali Baba as soon as the meal was finished.

Morgiana served the dinner, and saw that the supposed oil merchant had a dagger in his clothing. She retired, and dressed herself as a dancer. Then, taking a tambourine in her hand, she went before her master and his guest, and bowed.

She began to dance, which she could do very well. As she circled round the room, she drew a dagger, and flourished it here and there, as if it were part of the dance. Then, when she finished, she ran to Ali Baba and held out her tambourine to him.

He put in a piece of gold. She turned to the oil merchant, and held it out to him, holding her dagger in the other hand —then, before he knew what was happening, she struck him to the heart, and the wicked man fell dead before her.

"What do you mean by this!" cried Ali Baba in a rage. But Morgiana, stripping off the Captain's beard and outer garments, showed him—the Captain of the robbers.

"Now you are indeed a clever maid!" cried Ali Baba. "You shall marry my nephew, and I will set you up for life!"

"Come and see the jars that the merchant brought with him," said Morgiana. Ali Baba praised the clever slave with all his heart when he saw how she had saved him and his family from destruction, and at once caused her to be married to his nephew, who, on his part, was delighted to have such a pretty and clever maiden for his bride.

Ali Baba and his sons lived in wealth and happiness all their lives, using the treasure cave whenever they needed more riches, for now that the robbers had been killed there was nothing more to fear.